CW00708971

BUILD
UNIVERSES

Marétha Marais

Fat Boy No More

europe books

© 2021 **Europe Books** | London
www.europebooks.co.uk – info@europebooks.co.uk

ISBN 979-12-201-1122-5
First edition: July 2021

Distribution for the United Kingdom: **Vine House Distribution ltd**

Printed for Italy by Rotomail Italia
Finito di stampare nel mese di luglio 2021
presso Rotomail Italia S.p.A. - Vignate (MI)

Fat Boy No More

Year 1, Month 1, Week zero.

"Fat Boy! Wait up. We wanna talk to you."

That is me. I am a fat boy. I am fat. Overweight. Big-boned. Obese. Call it what you like, but I am the fat kid, the one who is supposed to have a lollipop in the mouth and be funny because he is fat. I'm neither. No lollypop or funny. I continue walking. Maybe, just maybe, this time they will leave me alone if I keep walking – no such luck.

Big Henry gets right into my face, his bubblegum breath hot on my cheek, his arms heavy around my shoulders.

"Hey, Little Nuke! When are you going to explode?" He wriggles his free hand's fingers in front of my face. "Kabooch! Guts all over the place."

This little nugget of wisdom sets his two followers, Dumb and Dumber, off and they start to laugh. Peter Wentworth's high pitch braying mixing with the snort and hiccup laugh of Gavin, 'The Crunch' Becker. For a twelve-year-old, this kid is ginormous; he even outsizes Big Henry. What he makes up in brawn he lost in brains out on the Rugby Field.

Fantastic, the only time these guys attend a History period, it has to be the day we learn about the bombing of Hiroshima and Nagasaki. The nuclear bombs were called Little Boy and Fat Man. Who would have thought that Big Henry can actually pay attention in class? I heard the snickers and giggling during class and saw the grins and now I know why – a brand-new nickname.

I continue walking. Big Henry puts his arm around me, pulling me close. My shoulder just the right height to fit into his wet, smelly armpit. He pokes my stomach with his finger and bursts out laughing when it jiggles.

"Look boys, Little Nuke is made of Jell-O."

I try pulling in my stomach and pushing away the poking finger, but he is not called Big Henry for nothing.

"Aww… no hiding the nuke." He keeps poking. I try to wriggle free, but Big Henry has some serious juice, and I have to endure the poking, prodding torment.

"Let me go!" My shout is muffled by his arm around my head. He tries to get a grip on my hair. I silently thank Dad for his short hair policy. I keep twisting and turning trying to escape, my breath coming in short gasps, my vision blurs, my arms too tired to push against his weight. Suddenly I'm free, the hooting of the school bus has put a stop to the torture. The three have to run to catch the school bus to another rugby-mad school in the West Rand. Big Henry is not one to waste an attentive audience, his parting shot makes them roar with laughter.

"Bye-Bye, Little Nuke, don't ya stuff your face so much that you go nuclear tonight." Peter Wentworth is laughing so hard that he misses a step and nearly falls out of the bus. Through the bus window, I can see The Crunch blowing up his cheeks, his fingers mimicking an explosion.

One foot in front of the other. Step. Another step. Step. Step. I so hate being fat. Hate it. Step. Step. Hate the fat jokes. Step. Step. I. Am. Not. Little. Nuke. Step. Step. I'm sick and tired of being called names. Step. Step.

"If you want to win the lotto, at least buy a ticket." One of my dad's life lessons pops into my head. Just whining about being fat is not going to make me lose weight. I have tried losing weight before. It was hard. After two weeks of eating nothing but salads and measuring each bite, I had enough and gave up. I did not even lose a single kilogram. Maybe this time it would be different. I have a secret weapon called Jamie Oliver, celebrity chef extraordinaire.

I was watching TV when I saw this program where Jamie Oliver was trying to get kids to eat healthier at school. He made it look so easy, not only were there delicious looking salads but also bread and pasta, even cakes and desserts. Just thinking about it makes me hungry.

"Hi David, are you ok?" Jennie's voice broke into my depressing thoughts. Jennie is the only one who calls me David besides Grandma Edith. She is the most beautiful girl in the whole school. Her slightly Asian features, exotic and different. Today her dark straight hair hangs in a braid over her shoulder; she totally rocks the pink bicycle helmet.

"David?" She sounds worried, leaning forward over the handlebars, her caramel brown eyes fixed on my face.

I suddenly realise that I am staring at her. I'm such a fool. She must think I'm a complete doofus. "Hi, Jennie. Yeah, I'm ok. Just thinking, you know." I nervously wipe my hands on my pants and self-consciously pull in my stomach.

She leans forward and touches my arm. "Henry is such an ass. Don't let him get to you. I'm sure by tomorrow, everyone will have forgotten about the silly nickname." She tries smiling, but the worried look stays in her eyes. We both know it is a lie to make me feel better. It's going to be a long time before anyone forgets about 'Little Nuke'.

"No worries," I lie right back. "I'm used to it. I'm just fine." I start to walk again. I do not want to see the pity in Jennie's eyes. "I'll see you tomorrow," I call over my shoulder and start to walk as fast as I can.

When I reach the corner, Jennie is still standing at the side of the road. She gives me a small wave when she notices me looking back.

That's it. I'm buying a ticket. I'm going to win the weightless lotto. Fat Boy, no more.

Year 1; Month 1; Week 1

Captain David Zacharias Log
Stardate 70985.9. Log Entry 114. Week 1.

Week one of my weight loss programme sucks big time.
And this is most probably going to be my very last entry.
I'm going to die once Big Henry finds out what Mom
and Dad are planning. I would not be in this mess and
soon to be dead, if only Mom had listened to me. Why
won't she help me? What is wrong with her? I do not know
what to do to make her listen. It doesn't matter though –
I'm going to be dead soon and still fat.
A dead fat kid.

I'm in the supermarket with Mom, pushing the trolley
up and down the aisles, while fighting a losing battle.
"Mom, I'm not going to drink Cola anymore, and I don't
want to eat sugar cereal in the morning."

"Yes, Honey" Mom answers. I just know she is not listening when she puts Coco Pops in the trolley.

"Mom, I'm serious!" I swap the Coco Pops for Kellogg's Cornflakes and Rice Krispies.

Mom just smiles and continues on her way. At the Cola,
she asks: "Which one?"

I shake my head. "No Cola. I'll drink water… or tea."

"Tea! You do not drink tea. Ever." She takes three Co-
las from the shelf and adds a Cola Lite, winking at me.
This is going to be tough. I try adding some fresh fruit and
vegetables, but Mom switches it out for canned fruit and
frozen vegetables. The trolley is filling up with sugary
goods, cakes, and bread. I've lost the battle before it even
began. Why doesn't she understand? I'm trying to lose
weight. She is my mom - she is supposed to help me, not

make my life miserable. It is not as if she can afford just to eat anything – she is also fat and moaning about it to her friends. Why is she not helping?

I slam the car door close as hard as I can. I refuse to even look at her. A chocolate bar appears in front of me. Gooey golden, sweet on the tongue caramel, enrobed in smooth, rich, dark chocolate.

NO! I do not believe this!

"MOM! Are you deaf or something?!" I grab the bar and using both hands, squash it into an unrecognisable shape, and throw it out the window. I'm so angry at her. "You are not LISTENING to me. Why are you not helping me? Do you want me to be fat? To get called names at school?!" I slam my fists onto the dashboard over and over again.

"Davey, calm down. It is ok. Mommy will talk to the principal."

I choose to ignore her. She's not listening to me, why should I? She covers my clenched fists. I struggle to free my hands. In the end, she let me go. I fold my arms and stare out the car window the whole trip home. I'm so angry. When we reach home, I jump from the car and run to my room. It feels good to slam my bedroom door and then lock it to keep her out. I turn on the stereo, Shaun Jacobs *Like Fire* blasts out, pushing at me, the drumbeats vibrating in my chest. Only then do I start crying.

Much later, I turn down the music and put on my headphones. I pull up my latest river town on the PC and start measuring and drawing in the stands on the northern town extension. These are going to be smaller stands for first-time homeowners, maybe retired people that want to be close to the shops and hospitals. I'll make some larger stands for parks and open spaces. Perhaps I should leave in the wood area to the south then they can go hiking for exercise.

I am going to be a town planner one day – design new towns for people to live in.

I can smell dinner all the way up in my room – mash, gravy, and chops. Mom is making my favourite comfort food. Most probably to make up for our fight. I can smell the meat – lightly roasted in a pan with sweet-tasting onions and garlic. Rich creamy brown gravy with bits of onion made in the same pan the lamb was roasted in. Maybe she will put in small white button mushrooms that would soak up the gravy turning a juicy honey brown. To top it all off; fluffy, buttery melt-in-your-mouth mash potatoes. My stomach rumbles in anticipation. My mom can cook, I sigh, the battle lost again.

When I hear the ringing summons of the bell announcing dinner, I rush to wash my hands and wipe my face. It would not go well if I'm late for dinner. We call it the Eating Bell. It was given to my parents as a wedding present by our dad's mother, Grandma Edith, with strict instructions to gather the family for meals by ringing the bell. It runs in the family – the German one that is. Grandma Edith was in the German military and lives by rules and more rules. I think Mom is afraid not to ring the bell in case Grandma Edith comes to hear about it and descends on our house in full German fury. That only happened once, and Christmas was cancelled that year.

It is just my luck that I run into Perfect Amelia on my way down. Amelia is my older sister, and of course, she is the only one in our family who is slim and athletic looking. Dad would be second on the scale with only a small belly pushing at his shirt fronts. Mine is larger than his. Mom and I are the big people in the family. We even look alike, both dark curly brown hair with brown eyes, and fat. Dad and Perfect Amelia are tall, blond, and have blue eyes.

She looks me over, flips her long blond hair to the side and in her perfectly modulated voice states: "You are in a heap of trouble. Broke the number one commandment I dare say. That is a hiding offence. You can be such a twit sometimes." She looks me up and down for a moment, then turns to descends the staircase. Perfect Amelia does not walk down staircases. She regally, hand on the railing, descends the stairs with grace. At the first landing, she looks over her shoulder at me. "Hurry, little brother, you do not want to add more offences to the capital crime."

She is so enjoying this; I scowl at her and follow her down. I have lost my appetite.

Our house has ten rules we call the Ten Commandments, and no, it is not the same as the ones in the Bible. This is the Miller Household Ten Commandments and messing around with the first five commandments will earn you a hiding. The Miller children have agreed to this. We sit around the table each year on Family Day, which falls on the 26th of December and the Ten Commandments are reviewed, but so far, no changes have been made. The first commandment is: *You shall not disrespect your parents.* It covers a multitude of sins, from lying to fighting with others. Shouting at my mom definitely falls under that one. I did not even help her to bring in the groceries. I am so going to get a hiding tonight. I cannot even defend my behaviour to Dad. When it gets to Mom, Dad is kind of deaf. He would just go: "Your mother – whack – is my wife first and foremost –whack- and by the grace of God – whack- she is your mother – whack – and you shall respect –whack – my wife – whack."

I slide into my seat while Mom is dishing up. "Mom, I do not want that much food. I'm trying to lose weight. I'll have the same amount as Amelia."

"You are a growing boy – you need your food" and Mom ladles in another spoon of shiny brown gravy with bits of onions and mushrooms adding to the healthy helping of buttery yellow fluffy mash potatoes. Heavenly smelling perfectly roasted lamb chops round out the evening meal.

"Please, Dad, talk to Mom – she is not helping!"

Dad shakes his head: "Bubbles, cut the boy some slack. If he is hungry, he will find food in the fridge."

Mom puts the heaped plate in front of me and pours a large glass of Cola. She puts her hand on my shoulder. "Don't worry, it is Coke Lite."

Defeated, I finished my plate, no reason to waste good food when it is already there, but I did not touch the Coke. Even the threat of a possible beating could not take away my enjoyment of the perfectly roasted juicy chop seasoned with rosemary, the fat both crispy and salty. The mash melting in my mouth and the button mushrooms are little bursts of flavour when you bite into them. Like I said, my mom can cook.

With my plate clean of the last bit of sauce, reality comes rushing back. I listen to Dad telling Mom about his latest project. Dad is an engineer at a government parastatal, they do lots of work funded by Denmark, and have new projects all the time. Dad once took me to his work and showed me around. I like the Town Planning Department the best. When Dad was called into a meeting, I spend an entire day with one of the town planners. He showed me how they layout towns with houses, businesses, roads and parks. Since then, I have been planning my own; a mixed-use river development. This is when there are both houses and businesses together in the same area – like in 18oo's. During that era, the shopkeepers lived above their shops. I wonder if the butcher also lived above the butchery; it doesn't smell nice. I would have liked to live above a bakery – waking up to the scent of freshly baked bread, raisin bread with a coat of melted butter to turn the crust on top brown, shiny and yummy. I love the smell of cinnamon, cardamom, and aniseed.

Mom gets up and starts to clear away the plates. I grab an empty dish and follow her to the kitchen. Perhaps helping out would score some points when Dad starts dealing out my punishment. I put cling film over the class of Coke and put it in the fridge. Mom shakes her head and starts stacking the plates in the dishwasher.

Amelia comes around the corner with the serviettes; she waves them in front of me: "Dad's asking for you. You may want to make a detour before visiting the lion's den." She looks meaningfully at the serviettes. I sigh and push past her; the time of reckoning is here.

No detour. I knock on the open door. Dad puts the folded newspaper on the side of his desk. He just looks at me without speaking. I wipe my hands on my pants and put them behind my back, locking my fingers together to keep my hands from shaking.

"Davey, how are we going to solve this problem?" Best not to say anything. Dad usually talks through a problem. Only when he reaches a solution are you supposed to answer. Dad starts his pacing. He is a tall man with a military bearing, four steps to the lamp in the corner, a brief pause, left turnabout and four steps back. "Our previous solution did not yield the desired results. In fact, it seems to have escalated." I stare at his back, there are creases in his shirt from sitting in meetings all day. He faces me again, his blue eyes, so very much like Perfect Amelia's, look me up and down. "We have to change our line of thinking, change our focus." I can feel the sweat gathering in my hairline. My legs feel kinda shaky, my stomach feels heavy. "Your mother, my wife, has offered a solution, but in my opinion, stronger measures need to be taken."

Six – that's how many whacks Dad usually deals out for Commandment One. I can take that. My backside clenches in readiness for the first blow.

"Davey, are you listening to me?"

Oh hell. Now Dad's going to think I'm ignoring him. When did he reach his solution? What is the answer? My head is a spinning black hole, any thoughts I may have had sucked into the dark abyss.

"I… I think it is a good idea," I offered nervously; I hope that I did not agree to be sold into slavery or being grounded for the rest of my life.

"Good, I'll ask your mother to set it up." He offers me his gold pen with the black band in the middle; the one Mom gave him for their wedding anniversary. Do I have to sign something? The pen is warm from his body heat. It feels slippery in my clammy hands – he holds out his red notebook. "Write it down." I have no idea what Dad is talking about. He puts the notebook down on the desk and opens it to a blank page. "The names, Davey, write them down."

Names? I stare at the white page with the grey lines. I did not call Mom any names… did I?

"Davey, sometimes you just have to face the situation and be the first one to speak up. Write down the names of the boys who are bullying you. We will meet with their parents. There is some truth in Captain James Kirk's philosophy… *"The prejudices people feel about each other disappear when they get to know each other."*

Since Dad is quoting *Star Trek*, perhaps, I should have followed Mr Spock's wisdom: *"Insufficient facts always invite danger."* It seems I have just agreed to provide Dad with the names of Big Henry and his followers. I'm so dead. Deader than dead. With no way out and Dad watching over my shoulder I write in his red notebook, probably for the last time in my life, the names of Big Henry, Peter Wentworth and Gavin 'The Crunch' Becker. This is the last day of my life.

I'm jittery, my stomach feels heavy, my head hurts – life is a bitch. I do not know who said that. I hate my life. Why did Mom not listen to me? If Mom listened and helped me, I would not be facing my death at the age of eleven years. I hate being fat. I hate this fat jiggling body. I look like a beached whale. A very white, fat-ass whale.

Mom knocks on my door. "Bedtime, Davey, it is school tomorrow. I made you some hot chocolate. You look pale, are you ok?" Mom puts the chocolate on the bedside table and reaches over to touch my forehead.

"Thanks, Mom." I pull away from her cool hand. "I'm fine – only tired, you know. Lots of schoolwork."

Mom starts to straighten my room. Folding up my T-shirt and putting my shoes in the cupboard. She checks my school shirt for tomorrow, smooth out the wrinkles in my grey pants. At the door, she pauses as if she wants to say something, then shakes her head. "Night-night Davey. I'll wake you at six, ok?"

"Good night Mom. Love you." That makes a smile, a real smile with the dimple in her left cheek. She blows me a kiss, and I catch it to my lips. I took the hot chocolate with me to the bathroom and dumped it down the drain while brushing my teeth.

Once in bed, I take out the black journal Grandma Edith gave me on my tenth birthday with the stern instruction to write in it as an orderly mind creates winners or something like that. My ten-year-old self wondered if Grandma Edith filed all her thoughts on data servers like in the movies. She wrote a poem on the first page called *Invictus* by William Ernest Henley. I have no idea what it is about, but the last two lines sounded like something that Captain James Kirk of the starship Enterprise would say: *"I am the master of my fate; I am the captain of my soul."* I decided to keep a captain's log; a diary is so something Perfect Amelia will keep. I tried to write in it every day, but I don't have that many thoughts that need to be organised. Not writing in it is not an option – it is Grandma Edith after all. So, I stick to once a week on a Sunday, but since it is most probably my last night on earth, I'm making an exception.

Year 1; Month 1; Week 2

Captain David Zacharias Log
Stardate 71005.0. Log Entry. 115 Week 2.

I am not dead yet. God must have listened to my prayers. Dad has several project deadlines, so Mom could not set up the meeting with the principal, and you know whose parents.

I'm still struggling to convince Mom that I'm serious about eating right. Quoting Superhero Jamie Oliver: "I'm not on a diet. I'm changing my eating habits." *Less of the bad foods and more of the good foods. My bad food list is short: no Cola, no chippies, no sweets. My good food list is very long, but healthy foods are an endangered food group in our house, few and occasional. We have tomatoes but no leafy greens. No beetroot or carrots. We do get some peas, but it is in a rich stew. Fruit is another problem – the battle continues.*

Week 2 sucks.

Year 1; Month 1; Week 3

Captain David Zacharias Log
Stardate 71024.2. Log Entry 116. Week 3.

I hate school. I wish it were the holidays already.
I'm not losing any weight, but I'm not giving up. I need a new battle plan to convince Mom that I'm serious about eating right; that is until I die and are eaten by wild dogs.
I'm still exercising, though I ache everywhere – even my butt is aching. I'm my own pain in the butt. I ride my bike in the garage; I'm not ready to leave and put on a world show. However, I'm quite sure that the strange kid from next door is watching me from his second storey bedroom window. He never leaves the house, so who is he going to tell? It was still distracting enough for me to hit the wall a few times when I thought I saw movement at his window. I can now do seven circuits – see gym term, I'm getting the hang of this exercise thing, even speaking the language.

My guardian angel is still looking out for me with Dad off to a conference in Cape Town, so the countdown for my execution by Big Henry is still on. I'm having nightmares where Big Henry grows to gigantic proportions and smothers me with his ginormous sweaty armpit. When I lie dead on the ground, Grouch and Peter turn into huge wild dogs tearing at my flesh. I usually wake up at that point all twisted up in my bedsheets. Once I woke up when I hit the floor. I'm gonna be so dead once Mom set up that meeting. This waiting is no good. Maybe I could tell Mom that they moved away. Yeah right, I can just see that eyebrow going up and up. I need a plan.

I'm in our garage, checking out my old bike. I have grown sideways more than lengthwise so I would most probably still be able to ride the thing. It looks sturdy enough to take the weight of a fat eleven soon to be a twelve-year-old boy. I close the garage door so that no one can see the show of a fat boy on a bike. I struggle to get onto the seat – my legs seem too short for my butt to reach the saddle and since I have no balance, I end up on the floor in a mess of arms, legs, bicycle, and I take a knock on the head from the handles. Finally, I figure out to lower the seat so that I can reach the pedals. With my first try, I went straight into the wall. Then the garage door, some boxes and after quite some time I complete a full circle of our four-car double volume garage without slamming into anything.

My legs are shaking. I have difficulty breathing; sweating buckets and am dead tired after five full circles with the bike. I have some scrapes on my knees and elbows also a raw patch on my face. My T-shirt sticks to my sweaty back and I smell bad.

"What happened to you?" I walk straight into Perfect Amelia in the kitchen. She's everywhere.

"Nothing," and I limp away to my bedroom. I just want to lay my tired body down on my bed.

"Mom! Davey has been fighting again! You should see him."

I hate Perfect Amelia! I wish she would keep her big mouth shut! Not long after I reach my bedroom, having to rest on each landing, Mom comes to check on me.

"Oh, Davey. What am I going to do? Munchkin, let me see where they hurt you. Mommy will make it all better. Who did this to you? That horrid Henry and his boys. I'm going to call the principal right now."

'Mom... Mom!" I can see she is not listening; she just keeps rattling on and on and on. "MOM!" Finally, she looks at me, a puzzled expression on her beautiful face. "I feel ok. Nobody else involved."

She does not believe me. She studies me like a specimen under a microscope. "Davey, you do not need to protect those boys. They are bullies and must be taken to task." She continues to wipe the dirt from the scratches on my knees and elbow. I should have worn my jeans and a long-sleeve T-shirt.

"Owww, Mom... I'm ok. I fell when I tripped over something on the sidewalk. I was not looking where I was going. I was thinking about something. I'm fine, do not worry. Please." I speak to the raised eyebrow. "I'm... I'm..." I need to think fast here. "...I was thinking about my new town, you know. It's a river town with mixed-use neighbourhoods... like olden times." The eyebrow wavers at the use of Grandpa Jan's favourite term. "People must be tired of all the glass and concrete. I think a village setup with wider sidewalks is better. I can add bicycle lanes, open spaces. Perhaps a community square for a market or something..."

Slowly, the eyebrow returns to its normal position. Mom shakes her head. "Oh, Davey, you are such a dreamer. You must be careful and alert when you walk home. You know Dad's rules. Be vigilant, be wary, be prepared to save the day." She smiles while reciting Dad's rule of the road. The dimple puts in an appearance. I have my suspicions that it is a more diplomatic version of Grandma Edith's rule of the road.

After a whole lecture about road safety and the dangers of living in South Africa, a big hug and a sweet from Mom (which I did not eat), I finally have some space to myself.

Year 1; Month 1; Week 4

Captain David Zacharias Log
Stardate 71043.4. Log Entry 117. Week 4.

I hate being fat. I am not going to give up. I'm not quitting.
The worst week of my entire life. Ever.
And to top it all – Mom. Why is she not helping me? Nothing! She does nothing.

My nickname is here to stay – I'm now called Nuke by nearly everyone. I hate every single one of them.

Jennie is the only one who calls me David. She has stopped twice on her way home to ask if I'm ok. I just smile and lie. She knows I'm lying. I can see it in her eyes. Tuesday was kind of bad, and she looked like she wanted to cry, but I made some stupid joke. She laughed, but her eyes did not light up. Her eyes are like my mom's dimple, only showing up when she is really smiling. Jennie made the day better.

I'm lying on my stomach, as my aching ass is now also a burning ass. I trespassed on the First Commandment, disrespecting my mom, and continued to sin through all the Commandments – right down to number ten – *shirking my duty as a member of the Miller household*. Sometimes I wish I belong to a family where they eat proper food. Unfortunately, I spoke my mind on that one too, so the punishment took place in instalments.

I'm angry with Mom. I'm trying so hard to change my eating habits, but she just keeps on pushing the bad foods. No vegetables, no fruit, no lean meat. Nothing! I was so mad. I screamed at her, and then Dad got involved, and everything went from bad to worse. Why is she so obstinate? A new word Dad called me: obstinate and disrespectful.

I'm still angry. My hand is shaking. In frustration, I throw the log and the pen across the room. I grab a pillow to stuff my face as I scream, Dad's home, after all. I bite and tear into the material, my breathing harsh in my ears. I jump up; it is not enough. I want to hit something. Anything. I kick the plastic wastebasket, it hits the wall, coming down it smashes into the photo frame it falls to the floor, the glass splintering in all directions. That makes me even angrier. I kick the basket again. It bounces off the door and rolls back to where I am standing. I keep kicking and kicking until I'm bending over, out of breath. My legs heavy, my throat burning, my teeth clenched tightly together. Snot and tears are running down my face. I did not even realise I am crying. My legs give out, I fall to the floor. I'm still angry but too tired to do anything more than taking a swipe at the misshapen basket. I just lay there, a big fat heap of nothing.

It is dark when I wake up. I drag myself to bed and pull the covers over my head. I'll deal tomorrow. I cry myself to sleep.

Year 1; Month 2; Week 5

Captain David Zacharias Log
Stardate 71062.6. Log Entry 118. Week 5.

Operation code name: White Whale.
1) Stay alive – Setup a new school events calendar for Mom and Dad to read.
2) Eat right – Tell Mom about Jamie Oliver. Amelia convinced Mom to buy some fruit – apples, oranges, and bananas.
3) Lose weight – And here is the kicker. Despite the lack of good foods, it seems by not eating sweets, chips, and not drinking Coke, exercising with the bike and the bottles, I think I might have lost some weight. My grey school pants seem to fit a bit more loosely. I'm not going to be fat anymore – it is just going to take longer than expected. I am the master of my fate; I am the captain of my soul. *But I'm still going to look like a white whale coming December.*

I wake up early and clean up the mess of the night before – no sense in getting into trouble for this too. Breakfast is a quiet affair as I refuse to speak to them. They are not listening to me, so why must I talk to them? Perfect Amelia decides today, of all days, to walk to school with me. She usually catches a lift with one of her giggling friends. But not today. Luckily, she is keeping her opinions to herself. I'm listening to Shawn Mendes on my buds. His *Show You* is my theme song for the day.

Do I need to show you?
Guess I gotta show you
And if you don't believe me now
I'll flip the whole world upside down…

When the school comes into view, I stuff my earphones in my bag before Big Henry helps himself to another pair. I turn into the school gate. Perfect Amelia suddenly grabs my arm "Davey, stop. I want to…" I pull away. So not talking to her, but Miss Perfect does not give up. She jumps in front of me and gets right into my face. "I want to help. With the dieting, if you are serious about it."

Why does everyone think I cannot do this? I stare straight back at her blue eyes with the surprisingly long dark lashes. She is so bloody perfect. I hate her.

"Say something, anything…"

I am not going to talk to her. A quick sidestep and I'm swallowed up by the crowd – a giant white whale bobbing in a wave of blue and red blazers. I can feel her eyes boring into my back of my head until the blue wave spits me out around the corner.

The rest of the week sucks as usual. My guardian angel is working overtime as I'm not dead yet. Big Henry and the wild dogs are away on a rugby camp, so the countdown continues. I might come up with a plan that I will put into action closer to the time. The School is planning an Outreach week with the community and social activities; we must bring old clothes, food (not old) and toys to school. People are also going to talk about how to help disadvantaged people and to get involved in charity events. There is even one for pets and animals in distress. I've decided to add bullying to the event calendar. That is where it gets tricky – I must make sure that Mom and Dad read my events calendar, not the one from the school. I must replace the school calendar with mine as soon as the school posts theirs. Timing is everything. I just need to make

Mom and Dad believe that I will speak up about being bullied.

On Thursday, Amelia barges into my room. Before I could tell her to leave, she dumps two 500ml bottles filled with water on my desk. While I'm trying to wrap my head around the concept that Amelia is in my room for real, she grabs the bottles and pushes them into my hands. She starts babbling about arm curls for my biceps and squats for my legs (like sitting down on a chair but without the chair). It seems Amelia has been using the bottles as weights like the bodybuilders. Not that she looks like a bodybuilder. Those bottles may look small and light, but after seven arm curls, they become pretty heavy.

"I'll save the Cola bottles for when you're ready," and she waltzes out of my room.

That evening in bed, I remember Amelia saying something strange. She said that if you lose weight too fast, you will just get fat again the moment you stop dieting. That is because you starved your body and now it will store the extra food for when you diet again. I did not know that, but it sounds like something Jamie Oliver said, *"Eating healthy is all about balance. You have to eat all the foods but in the right proportion."* That must be why Amelia stays slim as she eats the same food I do, just less, and she exercises. Maybe I don't hate blue-eyed, blond-haired Amelia so much anymore. I must tell Mom about Jamie.

Year 1; Month 2; Week 6

Captain David Zacharias Log
Stardate 71081.9. Log Entry 119. Week 6.

Operation code name: White Whale.
1) Stay alive – ongoing.
2) I'm creating a new school events calendar for Mom and Dad – progress is somewhat slow.
3) Tell Mom about Jamie Oliver – working up to it. Amelia has kind of a plan.
4) Lose weight – YES – I LOST SOME WEIGHT!!! My grey school pants definitely fit better. My shirt buttons no longer pull open so that you can see my white whale stomach. I can now fit into my Sunday pants. YES! When Amelia noticed that I could fit into my black pants, she gave me a thumbs-up sign. It made me feel good, even if it is still a battle when Mom continues to cook the most deliciously creamy, fatty meals.

"Why are you riding your bike in the garage? Do you not want to go outside? Are you grounded? Why is your garage as big as a house?"

I stop dead in my tracks. The boy from next door is hanging over the two-meter-plus high boundary wall, his skinny arms waving about as he talks. He looks like a puppet with a pale face and a mop of dark brown, nearly black, curly hair peeking over the wall. He continues to talk, his hands waving in the air. I keep staring, struck dumb by the situation.

"Hey!" he slaps the wall partly in frustration and to wake up from my trance.

Before I could speak, a woman's voice starts to pepper him with questions: "Adam McKenzie, what on earth are you doing up there? Who told you you could do that? Where did you get that ladder? Who are you talking to? What is going to happen when you fall?"

Like mother like son, question after question. When are you supposed to answer? Do they even want an answer? Adam looks at me; his brown eyes are full of mischief, his smile wide and carefree. The woman finally runs out of steam and Adam starts to fill in the blanks.

"I'm talking to my friend. His name is Davey. He is going to ride his bike with me. Tomorrow."

I am?

"Adam, get down that ladder, right now. Be careful." By the sound, she is moving closer, concern in her voice. "Slowly."

"I'll meet you at the gate tomorrow at four so that you can finish some of your homework first. Bye, Davey! Nice meeting you." And just like that, the Adam puppet disappears behind the wall. Only to pop up again. "I'll go slowly. You are not very fast yet." Then he is gone. Their voices fading in the distance.

I shake my head, what has just happened? Feels like I had an out of body experience, I was there but not there, no control over what happened. When did I agree to go riding with Adam? I'm very sure that I did not say a word. Perhaps I nodded at some stage...

At dinner, my confusion increases as Mom tells Dad that I am helping the sick little boy from next door. It seems Ms McKenzie called my mom and told her that I agreed to go biking with Adam tomorrow and she just wants to clear it with Mom since it's a school day. Mom beams at me, her smile all dimples. I try to tell her that she has it all wrong, but Dad is looking somewhat proud, and

34

for once Perfect Amelia is not getting all the praise and attention.

"Mom, would it be ok for Adam to be outside? He has not been in remission that long."

What is Perfect Amelia talking about? What is wrong with Adam?

"Oh, Megan says his health is quite good now. One-on-one interaction is safe. However, the doctors do not want him to go to school yet. He is still home-schooled. That is why Megan is so glad that Davey is helping out. It will give her some free time as she usually takes him to the park to ride his bike. His father, Iain, is not around much. From what I hear, he is quite a well-known attorney and goes away for work most of the time. You ask me - he is not coping so well with Adam's illness and is running away from his family when they need him so much." Mom presses her lips together, clearly not impressed with Mr Iain McKenzie.

I cannot contain my curiosity. "Mom, what is wrong with Adam?"

My mom looks sad, and Dad immediately puts his arm around her and gives her middle a light squeeze. He keeps his eyes on her when he answers. "Adam has an auto-immune disease. He was quite sick when he was a baby, but he is better now."

Dad continues to rub Mom's back. "I think he has been in remission for the last year or two."

Mum nods in agreement, her gold earrings catching the light when they swing with the movement of her head.

I like the way my mom dresses. She looks like the women in the pictures in Grandpa Jan's photo albums. Today she is wearing a dark blue dress with a full skirt that sways when she walks with a white collar and a dark blue belt. Dad's says Mom looks like a young Elizabeth Taylor.

I had to google it to find out who she is. She was an actress. There is a photo of Elizabeth Taylor on the web wearing a yellow and white check blouse with a white skirt that looks just like Mom.

"Yes. I think Adam's last episode was before his ninth birthday. He was still sick when it was his birthday. Poor kid could not even open his presents. He is such an adorable little boy; everyone is hoping he has outgrown the disease. I am so happy Davey has made friends with him. It will be good for Adam to have a friend closer to his age. He usually has to put up with all the old fuddy-duddies."

Mom is smiling again and I do not have the heart to tell her that I am not Adam's friend. I have not even talked to the kid, yet everyone thinks we are best friends.

Thursday rolls by and on the dot of four, Adam rings his bicycle bell at the gate. I really, really do not want to go bike riding in public. I dressed carefully in dark denim jeans and a long-sleeve T-shirt for protection, should I meet the asphalt. I'm wearing my red Converse for courage. "Hi, Adam." I wave half-heartedly.

He is wearing a blue bicycle helmet and even has blue and white pads on his knees and elbows. But the weirdest thing is his red ninja turtle body suit that protects his upper body, arms, and legs.

He sees me staring and starts to laugh. "It is called a G-suit and the only way that Mommy will let me out of the house on the bike." He looks me up and down. "Good thing too as I'm wearing enough for both of us." And off he goes.

"Hey! Wait up!" I start puffing after him. Luckily, he stops at the end of the block.

"Are we going to the park? Where do you want to go? Do you want to go to Mr Botha's house?"

Again with the machine gun questions. Adam looks happy all smiles and buzzing energy. I feel sorry for him, but there is no way I'm going down to the park.

"Adam – please slow down. I'm not used to riding my bike in the street. Give me some time to adjust to the idea, ok? For today, just around the block." I can see he is disappointed, but after looking, me up and down he seems to come to a decision and nods his head.

"Ok, for today. You need to wear a helmet anyway." Off he goes again. The little guy is quite fit, racing around the block without breaking a sweat while my legs turn to jelly and I can barely breathe.

"Hey, Fat Boy – you are slow. I want to go faster. What is wrong with you, you sound like the oxygen pump my granddad is using." He puffs-puffs through his lips to imitate the sound.

I stop dead. Furious, I turn to face him, eye-to-eye. "Adam, if you want to be my friend – do not call me Fat Boy. It is rude and insulting." I let him see and hear the anger in my face and voice. I will not be taunted by this little pipsqueak. I'm doing him a favour, not the other way around! The intensity and force of my anger shock him.

Adam opens and closes his mouth a few times with no words escaping. "I'm very, very sorry. I will never call you that again. Cross my heart. Please do not be angry. I will never ever call you that again. Please be my friend." Adam is close to tears; his face is all scrunched up his lips trembling, fingers curling and uncurling on the handlebars. "Please, Davey, I'm sorry. Really. Truly"

I look at the too skinny kid, with his over the top safety gear, the tears leaving wet marks on his cheeks and I suddenly feel guilty. He is just a little kid; I should not have shouted at him. Perhaps he did not realise how rude he has been. It is not as if he gets out a lot. "Ok, but you must promise to never ever call me fat again. I'm not going to be fat for very much longer."

Adam's still looks warily, but he has stopped crying. After a few sniffs and wiping his nose on his sleeve (yuck), his brown eyes start to sparkle again. "Then you will be able to go very fast. Can we go down St Michael's Avenue when you are no longer fat?"

I just shake my head and get on the bike again. "One day at a time, Adam. I'll race you to the corner."

I lose again.

I am so stiff and sore on Friday that I could barely walk down the stairs, only the fact that my school pants are fitting better, give me the needed push to be on my bike when Adam rang the bell at four. It is a good thing that I have Adam and his boundless energy. Adam has, in just two short days, become my secret training partner. Not that he knows it. I will not give him that much power. Adam is relentless, once he has an idea in his head, nothing can shake it. Take the obsession he has for going down St Michael Avenue. I just keep ignoring his comments. I'm not going anywhere near that mountain of a hill.

His mom does not want him to bother me over the weekend, but she was quite happy when I begged Mom on Sunday afternoon to call and ask if Adam wanted to go for a bike ride.

I needed some exercise after our huge Sunday meal. Lunch was crispy fried chicken served in a creamy white wine sauce with nutty brown rice. Served with sweet carrots and green peas made shiny by a good spoonful of butter. Potatoes fried to golden perfection. Crunchy on the outside and soft in the inside with a generous sprinkle of Aromat and feta cheese. It was very, very tempting and hard not to ask for a second helping. Don't forget dessert

– deep orange pumpkin fritters drizzled in a creamy caramel sauce with a scoop of vanilla ice cream. I could just feel how my stomach slowly expands to fill up the little bit of space created in my black Sunday pants waistline.

I did four laps around the block and Adam six. He has no patience with my slow pace and would race ahead, catching me up from behind. In fact, it is quite embarrassing, Ugh, now I'm hungry again just thinking about the delicious chicken… and pumpkin fritters. Finger-Lickin goodness.

Year 1; Month 2; Week 7

Captain David Zacharias Log
Stardate 71101.1 Log Entry 120. Week 7.

Operation code name: White Whale.
1)Stay alive – ongoing.
2)Setup a new school events calendar for Mom and Dad
to read – still need a bit of tweaking but nearly done.
3)Tell Mom about Jamie Oliver – DONE. Mom is all
in.
4)Lose weight – On track – and I'm going to lose even
more.

On Wednesday, I notice that Mom only put a jug of water with lemon and cucumber slices in it on the table. No more Coke. Since the huge blow-up a few weeks ago, nobody dares to say anything about food. You eat what is on your plate. Dad is taking no prisoners. But Mom is serving water; perhaps, the time is right to introduce my secret weapon – Jamie Olivier.

I try to catch Amelia's eye as she is supposed to be helping me, but she is talking to Dad about going to a party with her boyfriend. Now that she is sixteen, she may go to parties if Mom and Dad have met the parents. I do not like her boyfriend – the guy is so over-friendly and worst of all – he plays rugby. I once caught the two kissing in the kitchen. It was soooo gross. Perfect Amelia went red in the face. She needs a new boyfriend as simple as that.

"Mom, if Amelia is going out with her sucky boyfriend on Friday, can we watch a movie together?"

Dad rarely watches movies and then only movies with subtitles. Mom calls him a movie snob, but still watches movies with Dad, just not the war stuff. Dad is a war movie fanatic; it must be because he has Grandma Edith for a mother. And his dad. And Grandfather – hell, the whole Miller family is in the armed forces. Dad was a soldier in Germany before he immigrated to South Africa. One look at Mom and he lost his heart on the spot and decided South Africa is his new home. Grandma Edith was and is still very unhappy about Dad's decision to stay in South Africa. Says he has deserted the family. Wonder if that means Dad has trespassed on commandment number ten – *shirking his duty as a member of the Miller household* and all that. I wish I knew what penance he had to do for that. Most probably a thousand push-ups with Grandma Edith standing over him counting: "Eins... zwei... drei... vier... fünf..."

"Sure honey. Don't call Amelia's boyfriend names, it is rude. Bernard is a perfectly nice boy. I'll order in some pizzas since it will only be the two of us. Hank dear, are you still going to the church meeting?"

Dad is on the building committee for the new church expansion. Those church meetings go on forever. Dad says too many opinions, and no one has the guts to make a decision. He is going to be quite grumpy when he gets home. He also hates pizza. I just hope my plan to introduce Jamie Olivier goes off smoothly.

"No, you can't have Jamie's pizzas on Friday. You promised we could try them together. Mom, this is not fair – please tell Davey no." Okaaaay. Now I know what they mean when they say women can multi-task. Amelia's talking to Dad and listening to Mom and me talking. I'm keeping my fingers crossed and for good measure, my ankles too. I hope that this is going to work.

"You are going out with smoochy Barney on Friday – Mom and I can eat what we like." I make kissing noises.

"His name is Bernard, and you are so ill-mannered. Mom, could we please have Jamie's pizzas on Saturday? I'll help you with everything. Please, Mom." Amelia turns her big pleading blue eyes on Dad, both hands on his arm. "Please Dad, I guarantee that you will like Jamie's pizzas; it is not an oily cheese riddled soggy mess. Promise."

Wow, she's good, even Dad seems to consider the idea of a Jamie pizza seriously.

"Is Jamie's a new pizza place? When did it open?" Mom is the one to ask the crucial questions. I let Amelia take the lead since she turns out to be such a perfect actress.

"Oh, no, Mom. It is not a place; it is Jamie Oliver, the chef on TV. Davey was watching a re-run of his cooking show. Jamie made his own pizza dough and then put the most delicious toppings on it. He made a breakfast pizza with a whole egg, tomatoes, olives, and basil and even a dessert pizza with red and green grapes topped with ice cream."

Good start with the sweet stuff – Mom looks cautiously interested. Dad, on the other hand, looks unconvinced, not impressed by the toppings on offer. Amelia, noticing his expression, hugs him. "Dad, you can put anything on Jamie's pizza dough – even sauerkraut and pulled pork. And cheese is optional." She pushed the right button. Jip, my sister, is perfect.

Dad gets a calculating look in his eyes. "Sauerkraut, beetroot and Danish feta."

Mom joins in: "Pears, figs, honey, a sprinkling of nuts with orange shavings rounded off with brie cheese."

"Sweets for my honey. I might even have a bite of that." Dad does his goofy smile and kisses Mom's hand. "Would making the dough not take a long time?"

Mom shakes her head. "No, not that long, about forty-five minutes I would say and a minimum of one to two hours for resting the dough. Amelia, do you have the recipe that this Jamie Oliver is using for his pizzas?"

"Mom, you can also get ready-made pizza dough from Geneva Bakery, but you have to order it." Mom gives me a strange look. "Hey, it says that in the window above the gingerbread men. You can barely see the little men so big is the sign. I had to buy a cookie to give as a birthday present."

Everyone is now looking at me. I can see relief in Mom's eyes that I have decided to end my diet fad and disappointment in Dad's because I failed again.

Perfect Amelia to the rescue. "That so sweet. What did Jennie say? Hope you at least put it in a gift bag." Thanks, Amelia, now I am in even more trouble. I'm sure my ears are burning red.

"Who is Jennie?" Typically woman, Mom wants the details and Perfect Amelia is happy to tell it all. How does she know so much?

"Jennie is Sunny's younger sister. You remember I told you about the Chinese girl in my grade – May Chen? Jennie is her younger sister. I think she is in a grade below Davey. Sunny says Jennie always talks about Davey since the day she met him at school. Davey is her hero – he saved her when she got lost on her first day. She took a wrong turn and was walking in circles when Davey found her. He was so sweet; he held her hand all the way back to her classroom." Amelia is enjoying this way too much.

"She was crying, what was I supposed to do, leave her there?" I glare at Amelia, but she just smiles angelically.

"Davey, the hero of lost little girls."

Mom hugs me. "Leave Davey alone. He is always willing to help, like his dad. I'm so proud of you for helping

Jennie and Adam." Mom keeps hugging me. "Our Davey is growing up. He'll have a girlfriend one of these days."

I dare to glance at Dad, hoping to see something else besides disappointment in his eyes. He looks kind of proud and panicky at the same time. I wonder what I did now. My dad can be so strange sometimes. I finally managed to wriggle free of Mom's hugs. "Mom, Jennie is not my girlfriend. I barely see her at school." That is not a lie – I usually talk to her on my way home. Now, Dad is looking relieved. It must be a German thing.

On Friday evening, I set the TV on the BBC channel. Now I only need for Mom to be watching TV when Jamie Oliver presents his cooking programme. Everything is ready. Big juicy meaty hamburgers with thick-cut tomato slices, cheese, and sweet chilli sauce on lightly toasted sesame seed buns are waiting on plates piled high with crispy golden chips. The only concession made to my weight loss is that I'm sticking with one burger and Mom and I are sharing the chips. I'm having coffee and Mom a Savanah Dry. The food smells delicious, and I have been sneaking a few chippies while waiting for Mom to get off the phone. When I came back from fetching the drinks, Mom is busy watching Jamie explain how to make roasted tikka chicken, potatoes, and cauliflower. Score one for Team Davey. I put down the drinks, take a hungry bite out of my burger, and speak around the food in my mouth. "I would rather go with pumpkin."

"Don't talk with food in your mouth. Since when do you not like cauliflower?"

Mom does not sound angry, just puzzled, her eyes on the TV where Jamie is taking out a hot tikka chicken from the oven, the steam curling into the air. You can see and hear the food bubbling away. Good thing we are eating dinner as my mouth is watering for a bit of that chicken.

"Maybe my taste buds need a new cauliflower experience." Out of the corner of my eye, I watch for Mom's reaction. So far, so good.

She put her burger down and turn to look at me. "You are not going to let go of this diet thing, are you?"

"No. It is already working. I can fit into my black Sunday pants. Even my school clothes are fitting better. I can show you." I cross my fingers, waiting for Mom to speak.

She is smiling, the dimple playing hide and seek in her left cheek. "I know it is working."

"Mom?" She ignores me, her eyes fixed on Jamie. "Mom, what do you mean – you know?" She puts her finger to her mouth to shush me, intent on watching Jamie smacking a pomegranate with a wooden spoon to get the seeds out. As if that works in real life. I try to eat slowly and enjoy the burger while watching Jamie prepare an apple crumble cookie. Why is she so mysterious? If she knows I'm losing weight, why does she keep on pushing the bad foods? I make another attempt to get Mom to talk. "Mom, I do not understand."

Mom ignores the question: "Davey, put on the DVD, your dad is going to be home soon, and he won't be in a mood for *Mamma Mia* tonight."

I'm not going to win; perhaps, Amelia would be able to get to the bottom of this. Must be a women thing.

I liked the first *Mamma Mia*. The follow-up movie is rather sad, but that does not stop Mom and me from singing along. Mom has a fantastic singing voice, must be all that Irish blood. I can carry a tune, Perfect Amelia, naturally, has the perfect soprano voice. Dad is quite a surprise. For a tall, lean guy, he has a deep bass voice. I think he is sorta shy about it and only sings in church but refuses to join the choir with Mom. When the Irish part of the family gets together over Christmas, he plays the trumpet.

Dad arrives home while the end credits roll with Amelia in tow. That is another Miller rule – Mom or Dad always pick us up from a party, as they do not trust that the designated driver will still be sober at the end of the party. Amelia looks pretty in her white and silver blouse with a dark blue denim and silver sandals. Her hair is in a long ponytail and she is wearing long silver earrings, but she does not look happy. Usually, when she gets back from a party, she is bursting with energy and would talk a mile a minute, but tonight she is a bit down. "Night Mom, I'm tired, it was a long day. I'm going to bed." And before I could talk to her, she disappears up the stairs.

"Hank, did Amelia say anything when you picked her up?" Mom noticed it too.

Dad shakes his head. "No, she just said it was a lame party and she has a headache. Why do you ask? I need a cup of tea." Dad goes to the kitchen. Mom keeps staring up the stairs as if she can still see Amelia.

"I'll make her a cup of hot tea and give her two Panado tablets for the headache. Would you like some Milo, Davey?"

"No thanks, Mom. I'm fine." I just want to go upstairs and talk to Amelia about Mom's cryptic words. "Night-night, Mom." I give her a quick kiss. Halfway up the stairs, I remember and yell, "Good night Dad!" I did not hear his answer.

Amelia's bedroom door is closed. I knock softly. After a while, she opens the door. Her room is full of shadows; only her bed light is on. I think she has been crying. "Hi... I just wanted to tell you that Mom watched Jamie's show. The whole show. And I think she liked it."

"I'm glad, Davey. We'll talk tomorrow." Her bedroom door clicks closed. I slowly walk back to my room. Something is definitely up. I really wanted to talk to her, but now it must wait until tomorrow. It is so frustrating.

When Dad wakes me up at 8:00 on Saturday, it feels as if I have just gone to sleep. Last night I rolled around for a long time, too frustrated to fall asleep. When I did, I dream strange dreams all night. Behind every door I open, someone tells me that they know it is working. Even Jennie was there. When I tried to ask her what she means, Big Henry told me to shut my trap. My eyes feel all scratchy and I can't stop yawning. I barely had enough time to wash my face and brush my teeth before the Eating Bell sounds. Amelia's bedroom door is open; she must be downstairs already. When I get to the kitchen, Amelia is chatting happily with Mom. Whatever crisis loomed last night seems to have solved itself overnight. But she is ignoring all the signals I send that I want to talk to her.

"So, Davey, what do you think?" Mom is looking expectantly at me; somewhere I missed the plot.

"Ah... mmm... about what, Mom?" And of course, it is Ms Perfect who chips in to provide the missing clues.

"The porridge you are eating, Davey. Are you still sleep? Really, you can be so daft at times. Mom made a special breakfast today. You have already eaten half of it!" She dismisses me with a flick of her hair turns to talk to Mom. "I told you that the men in this family would not even notice the difference. We went to such trouble, and this is the thanks we get. I really do not know how women can do it day after day."

I look down at the bowl in front of me. At first, it seems like regular old breakfast oats, but then I see the banana and nuts, the yoghurt and the honey. I was so focused on

48

getting Perfect Amelia's attention and finally solving the riddle that I did not notice what I was eating. I look at Dad. Oh, he knows what he has been eating. He is busy doing that close eye thing called savouring the moment – the same one he does when he eats a perfect piece of chocolate or drinks brandy. No, help there – I'm on my own.

The yoghurt and honey make white and golden swirls through the creamy oats. Cinnamon lightly dusts the almonds, and bananas on top of the oats. I take a bite. The sour yoghurt and the sweet taste of the honey mix with the cinnamon and suddenly the usually bland oats is a taste sensation. The almond flakes add a little nutty crunch to the creamy oats. Oats tasting this good could not possibly be healthy.

"Well, do you like it?" Mom is still smiling, but I can hear the nervousness in her voice.

"This is heaven. I do not care if it is healthy or not." I do not want to talk. I want to eat my oats while it is still hot and creamy with the cold honey yoghurt.

"316 calories in total. It is a Jamie Oliver recipe. I added honey to the yoghurt as I know you like something sweet in the morning to get you going."

I just stare at Mom. How, when, and where did this happen? Did I sleep longer than just a single night? I do not know what to say.

"Say thank you, you twit, Mom made it especially for you."

"Thanks, Mom. Thank you for making it. Where did you get the recipe?"

"I know how to use the internet, Davey. I also know you set me up last night to watch Jamie Oliver."

I must look like a fish. My mouth opening and closing, but nothing is coming out. I look at Amelia, she pretends not to see me looking at her. She is eating delicate bites of her oats.

"Bubbles?" Dad is looking longingly at the pot on the stove, his now empty bowl in his hand.

"Sorry, Love, there was only enough oats left in the box to make four bowls. I'll get some more oats on Monday." Mom is positively beaming – she made us all eat oats and like it. My mom is usually the only one in the Miller household who eat oats. Whenever she dares to serve the gooey tasteless mix for breakfast, we all take a few bites and then rush off, as if we do not want to be late for some imaginary school project. I do not mind eating this creamy, tasty oats at all.

It is my turn to help Mom with the dishes. "Mom, are you angry about Jamie? I'm sorry I set you up. I just really want to lose weight. Jamie seems to know how to make it easier. You do not need to measure your food and... and it is normal food, you know. It is not as if you are on a diet. You do not have to buy special things to eat. It is just food – everyday food. Please, Mom, will you help me?"

"Oh, Davey, of course, I will" Mom puts her wet hand on my cheek and kisses me on the head. "You are so much braver than I am."

"I don't understand, Mom. Why am I brave? Why did you say that you know I am losing weight but still…?"

Mom put her hand over my mouth. "I'll explain." She takes the drying cloth from my hand and makes me sit at the table. Mom takes the seat across from me. "Davey, I have been trying for years to lose weight. I will lose a few kilograms, but as soon as I stop dieting, I gain all the weight back. When the weight comes back, I get depressed and start eating more, then I gain even more weight. At some point, I started using appetite suppressors, pills, and even injections. Some of the stuff made me quite ill. I eventually ended up in the hospital. It was then that your dad made me promise to stop dieting – he loves me just the way I am. Do you know what is strange, when there was no pressure for me to lose weight, I actually lost some weight. I'm still overweight, but it has now stayed more or less the same for the last few years. I was ok with it, sort of." She sighs. "Until you started on this diet of yours."

I want to protest that I am not on a diet. I want to make a lifestyle change. Mom holds up her hand, stopping the words from spilling out. She looks sad. "I know, I know – not a diet – a lifestyle change. What is going to happen when you decide to stop? I am afraid for you – I do not want you to have to deal with the ups-and-downs of dieting. I know that you got discouraged last time when you did not lose weight fast enough. It broke my heart." Mom takes hold of my hand and squeezes it. Her hands are warm from washing the dishes. I do not know what to say. I don't want her to be sad… or afraid. I'm scared too – what if she is right and all the weight comes back? I do not want to think about it. Mom rubs my hand. She is quiet for a while, wiping the clean table over and over again with the red-check drying cloth. When she starts speaking, it is so soft I can barely hear her. "This time it is different, you are so sure. So determined to do this, you are even fighting with me." She gives me a faint smile. "It has been weeks, and you still haven't given up. This makes me even more afraid and worried. First, I was so worried that you would get hurt when you did not lose weight that I wanted no part in it. Then you started losing weight, and I was even more afraid. Afraid that when you stop losing weight, you're going to give up. Then, without trying, I also lost some weight. So now I'm scared of what is going to happen when you stop eating this way and all the weight comes back." Mom stops wiping the table. She starts to fold the drying cloth in a big square. The big square is folded in half and the half in another half. She keeps folding until the fabric unfolds itself. Mom pushes it away and crosses her arms. She does not look at me.

I touch her arm. "Mom… it's ok. I'm ok." I still do not know what to say. I do not want Mom to be so sad and afraid. This is not my mom. My mom can do anything; she always knows what to do. I'm scared; maybe I should go get Dad, he would know what to do. I started to get up, but Mom starts talking again. I sit down slowly.

"I wanted to protect you and ended up hurting you. You must have been so alone. I'm sorry for not helping you, believing in you. I sometimes forget that you are also your father's son; you have his drive and determination. You know what – I think your dad is right. This time you are doing it for yourself. You are losing weight because you want to. You are ready for this, and I'm along for the ride." Mom cups my face in her hands. I look into her brown eyes – so like mine. I do not like the sad, half lost look on her face. I put my hands over hers. I want to cry. Where is my dad? Mom needs my dad. Even Perfect Amelia would be ok. When you do not need her, she is everywhere, now when she needs to be here, she is missing.

"Can you forgive me for being such a horrible Mom?"

Her question surprises me and makes me feel ashamed. All those things I shouted at her. I do not hate her.

"It ok Mom, everything is ok. I love you; you are my mom; I love you. You are the best mom in the whole world!"

Now, Mom looks like she is going to cry. I do not know what to do. In desperation, I hug her and keep on hugging her.

For a long time, I just sit at the table with Mom. It is so strange; I did not even realise that Mom also struggled with her weight. Looking back, I remember times when we were eating bizarre foods. One time we only ate soup. Day in and out. It felt like forever but must have been a week or two at most. Like the salads with leafy greens, tuna, and feta. That one lasted so long that I can identify and name all the different types of salad leaves on the market. I still hate tuna to this day.

"Mom, what do we do now?" I was so geared up for the battle that I never thought of what I would do when I won. I feel lost and unsure of what to do next.

Mom starts to laughs: "Now we change the way and what we eat. Slowly." Mom gets up and starts to wash the dishes again. My mom is back! She has made her decision,

"What are we going to eat, Mom?" I'm beginning to worry that we are now going to eat only salads and steamed chicken and vegetables. I want to lose weight but am not ready to starve for the rest of my life. That is too extreme.

"I started to read up on this Jamie Oliver when you continued to watch his programmes. He has a different way of doing things. You are right about normal food. What if the two of us look through his recipes and select the ones that fit with our lifestyle? Foods that are easy to get and make."

"Like the oats we ate this morning?"

"Hmm, and the pizza for tonight. Do not think for a minute that I did not know that you and your sister were up to something. When the two of you are not fighting, you make a good team."

I'm sure my ears are turning red, I busy myself drying the breakfast bowls. "I was desperate. It was like that bedfellow thing Dad always quotes."

"She is your sister, Davey!" and Mom smacks me lightly with the wet cloth. "It is: *politics makes for strange bedfellows*. Now scram and go do your homework."

When I woke up this morning, I was afraid that it was a dream. But it is really happening. Mom and I are going to help each other to lose weight. Saturday's pizzas are a huge success – even Dad is impressed. Mom decided to buy the ready-made dough at Geneva. Once she rolled out the four pizzas, she brushed over olive oil and covered them in foil until we need them. Dad learned a new word – portion control. No more seconds. He calls Mom the Portion Police.

Everyone made up their own toppings; everything looked so delicious that we all shared a slice or two of each other's pizza. Dad layered his with horseradish, sauerkraut, and pulled pork. I covered my base with tomato slices and added the pulled pork with crunchy red and yellow peppers. Mom made one with figs, cheese, honey, and pecan nuts – the perfect dessert. The strangest pizza was Perfect Amelia's. She started with a melted feta base. Then she piled on every leafy green she could find, drizzled it with balsamic vinegar, and finished with pumpkin seeds.

Amelia said that by using less fatty cheese, fresh vegetables, and fruit, we packed on fewer calories. I'm taking her word for it. I do not want to go back to measuring every single bite of food. I'm refusing to count calories.

While everyone was in such a good mood on Saturday evening, I asked for a new bicycle helmet – said I need it when I go biking with Adam. Mom being of good Irish stock naturally wanted to recycle Perfect Amelia's old bicycle helmet. It's pink, for heaven's sake! Not a bubble gum or neon pink, oh no. Miss Perfect had a fuchsia pink bicycle helmet 'artfully decorated with rhinestones' – her words. I'll rather look like a chipmunk with my squished up cheeks in my old helmet than subject myself to that horrid helmet. I'll die of shame. I do not even want to know what Adam would have said had Dad not saved me – he told Mom to buy me a new helmet that fits properly and also a reflector vest since I'll be riding in the street. Now I only hope Mom does not dress me up like a construction worker – yellow helmet and bright neon green reflector vest. For once in my life, I hope Amelia would interfere to save me from dying of embarrassment. Will have to wait and see what the lotto brings.

Year 1; Month 2; Week 8

Captain David Zacharias Log
Stardate 71120.5. Log Entry 121. Week 8.

Operation code name: White Whale.
1) APOLOGISE TO JENNIE – I hope she is at school this week.
2) Stay alive – not going so well this past week.
3) Setup a new school events calendar for Mom and Dad to read – done, not taking chances anymore.
4) Lose weight – At least this part is going well. My school pants need a belt.

A brand new week. We helped Mom work out a menu for the week using Jamie's recipes from the internet; eating the same food just in a different way. For breakfast, we are still eating Kellogg's All-Bran flakes or muesli but now with plain yoghurt and fruit like berries, apple, papaya, or banana. You can even sprinkle some nuts on top. I'm adding a little bit of honey as I'm not used to the slightly sour taste of the plain yoghurt, but it is growing on me. Dad says it reminds him of the Bircher muesli they used to eat. Mom also promised to make her super delicious oats on Wednesday and Saturdays.

We had a look at Jamie's healthy snacks for our lunch boxes. But the ingredients were, according to Amelia, 'a bit exotic' like kale, asparagus, flat bean dip, aubergines, and hummus. Yuck. Mom did not give up and found some nice ones. Like the pistachio, apricot & dark chocolate energy bars – can't wait for that one. Or the sweet potato muffins minus the chillies. Then there are the baked goujons. Goujons are strips of deep-fried fish or chicken coated in breadcrumbs or egg and flour – the healthy version is baked in the oven. Mom even found a recipe for a frozen yoghurt dessert.

I made Mom promise not to send me to school with a lunch box full of salad leaves. Today my lunch box has sweet red apple slices, rye bread with Marmite and Edam cheese, a snack bar, some raisins, and a small plain yoghurt.

On Tuesday, Mom made us pasta. She calls it Jamie's skinny carbonara. A gooey pasta with crispy bacon, peas, and garlic covered with basil leaves, parmesan, and crunchy roasted almonds on top. It was super delicious. Mom, as the portion police, made just enough so that we all eat the right amount of food. Amelia made a healthy salad with crispy iceberg lettuce; cooked beetroot, sweet, soft juicy pear slices, and white feta cheese. We went from a family barely eating vegetables to a five fruit and vegetables a day family. I'm not complaining at all.

I also noticed that while Mom is dishing up that her favourite light pink blouse with the blue polka dots is definitely not fitting so tight anymore. She caught me looking and gave me a thumbs-up sign behind Dad's back.

Why, when everything is going so well at home, everything goes wrong at school?

"Morning, Fat Face." It is only Wednesday and Big Henry is on my case again. I try to get past him and the wild dogs, but they are blocking the corridor.

"Let me go. What do you want?"

Big Henry pokes me in the stomach with his finger. "What's wrong, Nuke? You are looking a little pale today." Tilting his head to one side, he looks me up and down. "Wait for it." He holds his finger up in the air, Crunch and Peter watching him with doglike interest.

"Dare I say it? I have to say it. Boys, it looks like the Nuke is losing some girth." They all burst out laughing.

"Maybe his head is just looking smaller because his bottom is getting rounder." Peter Wentworth's joke starts a new round of laughter. Angry and embarrassed, I shove him out of my way, and he falls flat on his ass. That stops their laughter. Peter is a head taller than me and plays rugby. It seems my new exercise regime does have some advantages, but I have little time to feel good about my newfound strength.

"Miller, step into my classroom! Henry, you and your friends get to class. Right now."

"Yes, Mr Potgieter," and with a smirk, Big Henry and the wild dogs set off to their class.

"Now Mr Miller do explain to me your hooligan behaviour I have just witnessed."

I just stood there while Mr Potgieter went on and on and on. Finally, he let me go with a warning and a promise to call my mom and dad. I also got detention. I now have to stay late for two hours on Friday when everyone can go home and enjoy the weekend. I am so screwed. I can't wait for the holidays to begin. To make matters worse – Jennie witnessed the whole thing as she was in Mr Potgieter's class for Business Studies. I wanted to disappear into the floor, but magic does not happen in everyday life.

During break, I hide in the library. My stomach is in knots, anticipating the call to Mom or even worse Dad. This is really bad. It would give them a chance to set up the meeting before I could update the calendar. Everything was going so well. What am I going to do now?

"Hi, David, are you ok?" Jennie found me where I was hiding from the world.

"What do you want? Do I look like I'm ok? Why are you always on my case? Do you not have friends?" I did not even realise how rude I am until Jennie's shocked expression makes me go silent. She just stands there looking at me with this hurt expression on her face. Then she quietly turns around and walks away. It seems so unreal that it takes me a moment to figure out that the only person at school that talks to me are walking away. I try to go after her, but my foot gets caught in my backpack strap. I crash against the desk with a bang loud enough to wake the dead, my books fall out and my open lunchbox on top of that. Miss Gillian comes to investigate the commotion. I'm still trying to stand up, books, and lunch everywhere. Unable to deal with the mess, she just shakes her head and sighs: "Davey, please clean that up. I think you need to take a walk. It would do you good, relieve some of the stress, and calm you down."

The week mostly went downhill from there.

I waited for Jennie at the school gate to apologise, but she must have gone out the other entrance to avoid me. I feel horrible. I'm the lowest kind of low, lower than green slime in a dam.

On Thursday, I looked for her during class changes but did not see her. I waited at the gate again, but she did not show up. I'm sure Perfect Amelia will hear about this and tell Mom. Another thing to worry about besides the exams, the calendar, and the Meeting. My stomach is starting to hurt, I hug my middle hoping to lessen the pain. Perhaps I should man up and go to her house to apologise, but I do not know where she lives. I will have to ask Miss Perfect. Thanks but no thanks, I feel bad enough without Perfect

Amelia putting me down. I have to do something, anything. I keep listening for her bicycle bell the whole way home. I have never felt so alone.

It is an endless, horrible, awful week. I'm forever in trouble at school, and the nightmares are back. Only now, Jennie is also there. When Big Henry and the wild dogs attack me, she looks at me with a sad expression and then walks away. When I call out to her, she waves, wearing her pink bicycle helmet, and rings her bell. Then the wild dogs with their Crunch and Peter eyes are all over me; I breathe in their stinky hot breath while their teeth snap closer and closer to my neck. I usually wake up crying and covered in sweat. One time I was all twisted up in the bedsheets; I panicked and called out for help, but my throat was so dry, I croaked like a bull-frog and nobody heard my cry. I tried to find out her address without being too obvious and was so successful that nobody answered me.

I hope that she is at school next week; she cannot avoid me forever.

Adam is keeping my training on track, but I do need to get a bike helmet, he is getting impatient to go to the park. I promise him we can go as soon as I have a helmet. Must remember to ask Mom when she will pick it up... Additional safety gear would also come in handy at the speed that Adam is planning to go.

Year 1; Month 3; Week 9

Captain David Zacharias Log
Stardate 71139.7. Log Entry 122. Week 9.

Operation code name: White Whale.
1) APOLOGISE TO JENNIE – Finally managed to apologise but now I must go biking with Jennie. Every time I think about my twelfth birthday, I can hear the start of the Jaws *movie theme song playing. The sharks are circling closer and closer.*

2) Stay alive – still, a toss-up. Who is going to put me in the ground, Adam or Big Henry and the wild dogs?

3) New school events calendar – casually told Mom and Dad that there is an update and that I have downloaded and forwarded if they want to update their calendar. So far, so good.

4) Lose weight – My grey school pants finally fit me again like the day we bought them. Properly. I also graduated to 750ml water bottles and can now do 25 push-ups before collapsing.

"Slim, how fast do you think we can ride down St Michael Avenue? A hundred kilometres per hour? How fast can you go? You are bigger. Like a hundred and sixty?"

Adam and I are standing at the top of St Michael Avenue. While Adam is talking up a storm on how fast we can go down the awfully steep downhill, I'm contemplating the possibility of dying in an accident going down the tree-lined avenue. "Slow down, Adam. We have to build up to this – you know practice first with a small hill."

"But you said we could when you no longer fat. Your face is not so fat anymore, and you don't get so tired when we go around the block."

The kid looks like he is going to burst into tears – he really wants to bike down St Michael Avenue. To stop him from crying, I made him a promise: "Adam, I am still fat. I need time. Besides, we have to practice first. Get our legs stronger so that we can pedal very fast." I keep my fingers cross on that one. "And we have to make sure it is safe. Your mom will kill me if something happens to you."

That's to say if I do not die on my way down that street. I just hope the church at the end of St Michael Avenue is not for funerals for boys speed riding bikes down St Michael Avenue – straight into the graveyard.

Adam is not very happy and is quiet on the way back home. I try to cheer him up. "Adam, when we get back home, we will look on Google Maps to find streets we can practice on. We have to be scientific about it – like real athletes. They practice very well before they run a race. We must follow their example." That seems to make him happy. Sometimes logic and science is the only way to get Adam to rethink his position.

Once home, he could not get off his bike fast enough. His mom wants to know how the ride went, but he flashes past her up the stairs.

"Afternoon, Ms McKenzie. We went to St Michael Avenue today. Adam wants to look up some streets in Google Maps."

"That's ok. I'll bring the two of you some cold water. "Are you thirsty?"

"Thank you, Ms McKenzie, water would be nice. I'm quite thirsty." I can hear Adam calling; I wave to his mom before running up the stairs.

Adam is sitting in front of his laptop. "Look, Davey, I found two streets that we can practice on. And here is another one." I look over his shoulder. Luckily, the streets are not too far from here. "What about this one, Davey? It is not too far away. You are getting fitter by the day. Can we do this one too, please-please?"

I check the two new streets. They are in the opposite direction but still away from busy intersections – no schools or businesses in the area. The one is, however, close to a nursing home. We will have to watch out for the oldies in their cars. "Ok. That is five in total. Let's grade the streets from easy to difficult. Once we reach the most difficult hill, we will be ready for St Michael Avenue."

I better start saving for additional safety gear as I'm gonna need it as street number three has quite a steep incline and a sharp turn. Maybe even a G-suit like Adams. Between Adam and Big Henry, it is dangerous to be David Miller. Wonder who is going to get me killed first.

"Look, Davey, I numbered them. Which one must I put first? Mossie Street?"

Judging by the name alone, it might be a good starting point. "Yes, I think Mossie Street should be hill number one. Then we can do Loerie Street as it is in the same area but higher up so it should be steeper." Adam carefully writes down the hill numbers and street names. He draws a thick black line under the list and writes *St Michael Avenue* as if all the hills add up to just one – St Michael.

The next day, before school, I again wait for Jennie, but this time at the bicycle sheds. No sign of her yet – just like last week and yesterday and the day before. I have to do something; this is eating me up. I rub my stomach that is hurting again. I need to make things right with Jennie. Finally, she slips through the gate.

"Hi, Jennie." She nearly jumps out of her skin when I show up in front of her bike. The locking chain slipped through her hands and fell to the ground. I pick it up. "I've been looking for you since last week. I was very rude to you in the library. And I'm very sorry." The words come out in a rush. Jennie avoids looking at me. She is not talking either. I do not want her to leave, so I say the first thing that comes into my head. "This is an excellent bicycle lock. Quite heavy. I must get one for my bike too."

That catches her attention, she finally looks me in the eye. "You are now riding a bike to school?" She looks around to see where my bike could be.

"No, no, definitely not to school. It would not look good. I ride with a friend after school for fun."

"What do you mean it would not look good?"

I use my hands to measure my butt's width and hold the space over her bike seat. "The shape of things does not quite fit together yet. Like a round apple on a thin knife-edge." I smile at her. The joke is on me. For a moment, she looked puzzled; then her lips begin to twitch. She tries to hide it behind her tiny hands, but the laughter spills over into her eyes. When she stops giggling, I push again for an answer. "Will you please forgive me? I was in a bad mood and took it out on you. I'm very sorry."

She still looks a bit hesitant but then makes a decision. "Ok. I accept your apology. But because you made me cry, you have to go on a bike ride with me."

I did not hesitate. "Deal, but I'm asking for a rain check. Are you going away in December?"

"But that is months away – you only want to go biking in December?"

"Yes, so that there is time to make the shapes more cohesive." I move my hands in the air to demonstrate.

Jennie shakes her head. "No. October. You have to go biking with me the first weekend after your birthday in October."

For a moment I'm confused, how does she know that my birthday is in October? Then I remember Perfect Amelia knowing about my gingerbread cookie birthday gift. Jennie is holding her breath; I notice that she is standing on tippy-toes waiting for my answer. I do not want her to see this fat boy on a bike, but a twinge in my stomach makes the decision for me. "Ok, October it is." My reward is a beautiful smile, and then she grabs her backpack, walking backwards, watching me the whole time. At the gate, she stops:

"It is an Abus lock. You can get it online." Then she's gone.

Year 1; Month 3; Week 10

Captain David Zacharias Log
Stardate 71158.9. Log Entry 123. Week 10.

Operation code name: White Whale.
1) I'm starting to hate the idea of turning twelve. I do not want to have a party with sweets and cake that will mess up my weight loss. And the bike ride with Jennie…
2) Stay alive – the list of killers is growing: Sonny and her tiger swords, Adam and St Michaels and Big Henry and the wild dogs.
3) New school events calendar – no surprises yet.
4) Lose weight – Still on 25 push-ups and 20 squats. My legs are getting stronger.

The first thing I see on Monday afternoon, after my piano lesson, is a large box declaring that it has awesome stuff inside. Since my name is on it, I open it. Awesome stuff indeed. It is my new bicycle helmet – black with a red and white checked stripe down the middle. Thank you, Amelia. The box also contains matching black and red gloves and elbow and knee pads. I wonder if Mom may have heard about Adam's fascination with St Michael and thought I needed the extra protection.

"Mom! Mom, where are you?"

"Kitchen, Davey."

I give Mom a one-arm hug and kiss on the cheek. She smells nice. "Hi, Mom, what are you doing?" Mom is busy breaking open green pods and scraping out that looks suspiciously like peas into a half-filled bowl. Next to her, on the table, there is a whole bag full. When I press on a pod, it cracks open, the peas escaping all over the place.

"Hello, Love. How was school?"

"School's ok. Where did you get this?" I crack open another fat green pod and the peas scatter over the floor.

"Davey, you are making a mess. Hands off now." Mom pulls the bag away when I reach for another one. I like the crunch when it breaks like popping bubble wrap. "Clean that up – no, put it in the bin, and help your sister with lunch. I want to finish this."

"Are we going to have peas for lunch? Mom, you know I hate peas."

I hate the little round things with a vengeance, not so much for the taste but the endless effort to eat them. Spearing four of them at a time takes too long. Using a flat fork is not speeding things up either. First, you have to get the peas onto the fork. Then you have to keep it at a precise angle to prevent the green buggers from falling off while manoeuvring it into your mouth. Any miscalculation and the peas escape over the table and into the other foods. It is like the egg in the spoon race, and I'm not good with sports.

"No, Davey. We are having English muffins, tomato, and cheese for lunch. You can cut up the tomato while Amelia toasts the muffins." Mom continues to pop and scrape out the peas without a break, a smile on her face. "Tomatoes are waiting at the sink, one should be enough."

I approach the sink expecting to see the perfectly round red tomatoes, but on the sink sit four misshapen reddish-green lumps with green leaves at the top. It looks like someone has taken an orange and covered it with tomato skin. When I poke at it, the lump just squats there.

"It is called a 'beeshart' tomato. Fewer seeds, more flesh and much sweeter than the average tomato." Of course, Perfect Amelia knows the answer.

"I thought we are going to eat regular food. Not peas that need to be taken out of their pods or this strange thing that looks like a tomato dressed up like an orange."

"Beeshart, freshly plucked from the vine. The peas, too; they are called garden peas in case you are wondering."

"Your knife, little brother – slice away." I take the knife from Amelia and notice that she is holding a flat round greyish bread thing covered in a floury substance."

"What is that in your hand?"

"A whole-wheat English muffin. A high-fibre, low-fat option, extremely healthy for people who want to lose weight." When she cuts it in half, the inside looks like a dried out vetkoek. Lunch is looking less and less appealing.

I poke the lump with my knife. "Must I peel it first?"

"No, just slice it; most of the flavour is in the skin. They are already washed."

I took hold of the green bits at the top and twist them off. "Where did you get these? You know what Dad says: you do not need to buy stuff just because it is on a special." I reposition the lump on the cutting board, trying to figure out the best way to cut the thing. Lengthwise like a tomato or treat it like bread and slice if from the side – it is bigger than my two hands.

"We did not buy the vegetables, they were a gift."

"People do not give away food – there must be something wrong with it. You always say: do not take food from strangers. I'm not eating this." I put the knife down and step away from the beeshart thing.

"Davey, stop your nonsense. Tannie Kotie sends the vegetables and fruit from her garden." Mom does not look in my direction. Amelia is giggling away while cutting slices from a ball of mascarpone cheese.

If Mom looked in my direction, she would have seen me picking up my jaw from the floor. It feels as if I have arrived in a different time zone. An encounter with Tannie Kotie from three doors down does not leave any member of our family in a happy mood. She is the South African variant of Grandma Edith dipped in vinegar. Mom is usually in tears after talking to the old witch. Even Perfect Amelia's impeccable vocabulary includes some not so nice words while trying to get Mom to calm down.

Just to be sure: "Tannie Kotie from down the road?" Mom nods her head, her eyes firmly on the peas.

"Tell him, Mom, tell him what she said." Perfect Amelia has changed into the Energiser Bunny all energy and movement.

Mom suddenly looks shy, but she is still smiling. "She said that she has such abundance in her garden that she thought we would like some. It was very nice of her. She brought over all the vegetables and the guavas."

"That is not the whole story, Mom!" Amelia could not contain herself any longer. "I'll tell him. We met her at Fruit and Veg, and you know her, once she has you in her beady gaze, she does not let go. We tried to get away, but she caught up with Mom at the tomatoes. She told Mom right there in the shop to put the puny tomatoes down, she has much better tomatoes in her garden. She also took out the peas and the sliced pumpkin from our trolley. Can you believe it- such audacity? She even gave it to one of the shop assistants to put back where it belongs. Then she told Mom. You cannot even begin to imagine what she said so I'll tell you." She stops to take a deep breath, while Mom and I are hanging onto her every word. Mom is breaking a pod into little bits while watching Amelia. There are two red spots on her cheeks.

Amelia takes a deep breath, in a perfect imitation of Tannie Kotie, she tells the unimaginable fact. "Maeve, you are looking pretty today. That dress of yours fits so much better now that you have lost some weight. I'm glad you are finally looking after yourself and that dashing husband of yours. I noticed that your fat little boy has also lost some weight. He will never be scrawny, mind you, but you cannot have everything in life."

A backhanded compliment. One of her best. I look at Mom. She is wearing her dark purple dress with the yellow trailing flowers on the sleeves. Long gold earrings in the form of leaves hang from her ears hidden in her dark curly hair. My mom looks beautiful. In a very dark and secret corner of my mind, I must agree the dress does fit better.

"Mom always looks beautiful! That witch just does not want to say it." I give Mom a hug and a kiss. I feel a tingling all over, and now I cannot stop smiling – someone outside the family noticed that I'm losing weight! I try to downplay it, pretend that I did not hear it. "But I still do not understand why she sends us these strange vegetables."

Amelia gives an exaggerated sigh and explains. "According to Tannie Kotie's twisted mind, by giving us fresh vegetables and fruit, she can help Mom prepare healthy dishes and in doing so, save our family from obesity. She even gave Mom some recipes and told her that she would bring around vegetables since she has loads in her garden and knows that it will be for a good cause. And do not pretend that you are not pleased with the fact that people are starting to notice that you are losing weight." She does that hair thing and goes to take out the muffins that have popped out of the toaster all crispy and brown. She puts a piece of cheese on the muffins and holds out the plate to me. "The tomatoes go on top. Be quick so that we can eat while it is still hot."

In a daze, I take the plate. Taking up the knife, I cut through the beeshart tomato. The smell hit me – a green, earthly sunshine smell, slightly sweet and pure tomato. The inside is red with tiny seeds. It smells so good that I decide to sneak a taste. It is sweeter than the store-bought ones and much meatier, like a peach. Where the skin turns to green, it has a more tart flavour. Not bad at all. I cut up the whole tomato and put a thick slice on each of the muffins. The rest I leave on the cutting board to eat later.

Mom laughs when she sees the thick tomato slice: "Generous, I see. You like?" I pretend not to hear, looking for the paper towels to wipe my hands.

Amelia put some basil leaves on top and lunch is ready. We eat on the stoep. At least the English muffins look much better when toasted and do not taste like cardboard. All the strange vegetables aside – I like it and will eat it again. I'm losing weight without too much trouble and if the witch wants to help – let her, she has hurt Mom enough in the past.

On my way down at four to meet Adam, I detour to the kitchen all dressed up to thank Mom for the safety gear. Luckily, Amelia is nowhere in sight.

When Adam sees me, he says only one word: "Park?"

On my nod, he speeds down the sidewalk and hops down in the side street. I give chase. Luckily, some common sense makes him wait at the big four-way stop.

"Hell, Adam. Slow down, we do not want to get into an accident before we get to the park. Keep to the speed limit, we will get there."

"Yes, Big Brother. What speed limit is that – a snail or a tortoise?"

I smile at his cheeky comeback, still on a high from this afternoon's good news. "Behave, or I'll slow down even more."

Ten minutes and seventeen seconds later, we safely arrive at our destination. It is a municipal park but operated and managed by the Lions-Rotary Club, so it is in good condition and safe for kids to hang around in. At four in the afternoon, the place is quiet. Too late for the young ones, and too early for the adults that use the park after work. Since Adam knows the park, I let him take the lead. He follows one of the winding walkways down to the left and disappears between two hedges. He waits until I stop next to him. Tightens his helmet strap, unfasten, and fasten his gloves. Adam smiles at me give a yell, and takes off down the bicycle path – Adam McKenzie unleashed. His enthusiasm is contagious. I throw caution to the wind and race after him. The breeze rushing past is a welcome relieve on my heated face, and I feel alive and happy. In front of me, Adam effortlessly twists and turns through some obstacle course created with concrete cones, pipe halves, and steps. When he reaches the end, he punches the air laughing like a lunatic. He sees me and yells: "Common, Slim, you can do it. It is not that hard. Start slowly but not too slow, else you will fall."

Yeah, thanks, just what I want to hear. Well, I cannot let a ten-year-old upstage me, so I decide to try. Slow but not too slow. I wobble through the first four cones, then I sort of get the hang of it for the next three. I misjudge the distance, hit a cone and nearly fall off my bike while Adam is shouting instructions and directions. When I make the final approach and stop next to Adam, he gives me a thump on the shoulder.

"Told you, you can do it. I have been practising for the past year. You should have been here when I tried it the first time, Mommy was so nervous she made me fall and then she told me to try again. You wanna go again?"

"Let me catch my breath first. Drink some water, then we can go again." I'm feeling all superhero cool today and want to give the obstacles another try.

"Two minutes and forty-three seconds" I raise my eyebrow at Adam. "My best time for the Anaconda. Shall I tell you, your time?" He grins at me.

I'm going to hear my time regardless if I want to or not. "Yes, tell me."

"Four minutes and six seconds." But he is not done yet; I can see it in his face and the gleeful smile that lights it. "You want to know what my time was when I started. Must I tell you?" I nod, and he shows me his watch "Four minutes and fifty-three seconds. All the biking, round and round in your garage house made you good at missing stuff. If you practice, you can beat me." He suddenly frowns. "You never did tell me why your garage is as big as a house. Was the garage your old house before your real house? Is it haunted, so your dad built a new house? Who died there?"

"Adam! You'll stink at Twenty Questions. I cannot answer you if you keep running your mouth. Normal people ask one question at a time."

Adam smirks at me. "I'm not normal – I'm me. You still did not answer, not even one. Mommy says if you shake the bush hard enough, the dogs will scurry out. It means you will eventually answer all my questions. Sooooo..."

"Our house has always been our house. Dad made the garage bigger so that when we learn to drive, we can also park our cars in the garage and the top floor can be converted into a flat."

Adam seems disappointed with my answer. "No one died there? No ghost haunting the garage house? You sure? Did you ever sleep there?"

I put my finger to my lips and point as the obstacle course now named Anaconda, courtesy of Adam. He gets the message.

"Watch me!" He presses the button on his watch and takes off at sickening speed and my prayers that he must please not fall and break his neck. "Two minutes and forty-six seconds! Come on, Slim, show me what you got! I bet you are going to be faster now." Adam is jumping his bike up and down.

I make sure that my helmet fits snugly and tug on my gloves. Slow and steady, I'll just keep it slow and steady until I reach the end. The second time seems a bit easier now that I know what to expect. Still, a slight miss calculation going into one of the gulleys twists the front wheel to the side, I have to put both feet on the ground to steady the bike. A deep breath and I'm on my way again. When I finally clear the last cone, or fangs if you go the Adam route, it feels like I had run a race.

"Four minutes and one second. You lost some time when you stop at the belly button – you must jump them, not go through them. Wanna go again?"

No, thank you, twice in one day is enough for me. "This is my first time at the park – why do you not show me around? Slowly."

The rest of the hour, Adam shows me around the park. The Anaconda is his favourite place in the whole park, but he also likes to watch the kids skateboarding. I'm just glad to learn that his mom had put her foot down when it came to skateboarding. He can ride his bike and even do the Anaconda, but if he moans about a skateboard, all privileges will be taken away. The idea of Adam on a skateboard down St Michaels makes me break out in cold sweat. I send up a quick thank you prayer to my guardian angel and a levelheaded Ms Megan.

His mom is waiting at the gate for us. "Sorry Ms McKenzie, I forgot about the time. We went to the park for the first time today."

"It ok, Davey. I know how difficult it is to get Adam away from there. Did he show you the Anaconda and make you do a time trial? Did Adam ride his bike at the skateboard rink?" Her last words are muffled as Adam puts his hand over her mouth.

"Mommy, stop. You will stink at Twenty Questions. Normal people only ask one question at a time." I blush bright red when Adam repeats my words to his mom.

She wrinkles her nose and grins, just like Adam. "I like shaking the bush. Get inside young man, Aunt Gaby and Uncle Jo will be here at six-thirty." She pulls Adam's helmet from his head and combs her fingers through his matted hair while Adams wiggles around to escape.

"Do I have to eat with you? At the table? Uncle Jo smells funny. Is Father going to be here? You said he would come on the weekend, but he did not. Will he come tonight?"

Ms. McKenzie stops smiling. Her voice sounds funny when she speaks again: "Go and get ready, Adam." She pushes him in the direction of the house. One look at his mom's face and he goes all quiet and heads for home.

This is awkward. "I'm sorry, Ms McKenzie, I'll be sure to keep better time."

When I want to leave, she stops me with a hand on my arm. "It's ok, Davey. I'm not angry. I just want to say thank you for the time you spend with Adam. He can be such a handful at times. You do not need to go biking with him every day. Once or twice a week is ok. You even were so kind as to go with him on a Sunday. He misses his father, you know."

I'm not sure what to say. I do not want to tell the truth, that I'm using Adam as a training partner, but I need to say something; she is looking so guilty. "It is no trouble. I like riding my bike with him. He says funny stuff – we laugh a lot. It is really ok and no trouble at all."

Her smile is a bit crooked, but she is smiling. "Yes, Adam can be funny. You are such a sweet boy. Let me know when you need a break. I know you have exams starting soon." She gives me a little wave when I push my bike the short distance to our gate.

When I look back, Adam's mom is still standing outside their gate looking down the road. She has folded her arms around her body as if to hold the hurt inside. She seems smaller somehow, sad and lost. I do not want to leave her like that. "Ms McKenzie, please tell Adam by Friday three minutes and fifty-five seconds, and I'll jump the belly buttons." That makes her laugh. When she closes the door, I can hear her tell Adam that he has been challenged to a race. Ugh, what did I set myself up for? At least the park is on level ground and while we are chasing around on the Anaconda, St Michael's is not getting any closer.

I can smell bacon when I step through the door; dinner is going to be scrumptious. When the Eating Bell rings, I'm already halfway down the stairs. Dad trails in after Mom; the moment he sees me, he sends me a look that clearly says: 'Tread carefully, boy, I'm watching you.' Mom gently places the succulent pink salmon on the plates with a sprinkle of crispy bacon bits over the top. Then she uncovers the next dish – my first thought that it is some kind of spinach mush since it is so green. But the green is much brighter, you know, more like the colour of peas. I knew that peas were going to be on the menu, but Mom took it to an entirely new level. When I open my mouth to ask, Dad's foot hits me beneath the table. My mouth slams shut.

Perfect Amelia does the honours: "Mom, this is interesting. How did you get the peas like this?"

Mom looks quite pleased with herself. "It is one of Nigella Lawson's recipes – called mushy peas. I substituted the crème fraiche with yoghurt for a healthy alternative."

Amelia dips her fork into the peas and delicately tastes the green concoction. "I find it quite refreshing – the flavour complements the salmon and the salty bacon."

I figure the appropriate response, under Dad's watchful eye and tapping foot, is: "Mmmh, thanks, Mom," and stick to that throughout the meal. The salty bacon cut through the strong salmon taste, and if you add a small dash of the green mush, you could barely taste the lemony tartness of the peas.

Later that evening, I ask Mom about Adam's dad. "Mom, do you think Adam's dad will ever come back home?"

Mom is putting away the clean clothes. For a moment, I think she did not hear the question. "Why do you ask?"

"When Adam asked his mom, she looked sad. Do you think they are divorced but did not tell Adam?"

Mom puts the basket on my bed and sits down heavily. "Davey, that is Ms McKenzie's private life. No, they are not divorced, just separated for a while. Megan did hint that she thinks he is going to move back home, now that Adam is doing better. We can only pray that things work out for them. Davey, it is not your place to ask Adam about his dad."

"Mom, I did not ask anything. We were late, and Ms McKenzie said Adam has to hurry up because Aunt Gaby and Uncle Jo is coming to dinner. That was when Adam asked about his father. Adam does not talk about his dad at all. Nobody talks about him, even his nom did not answer him when Adam asked if he is coming to dinner or not,"

Mom gives me the folded clothes and points toward the cupboard. "Put that away and leave the McKenzie's to their business." Now she too looks upset. Her lips pressed into a thin line.

"Sorry, Mom."

At the door, she turns around. "Just be a good friend to Adam."

The peas should have been a warning that all good things come to an end.

While slowly making my way home on Tuesday because I am so stiff (my arms and shoulders are aching from the Anaconda time trials), I get to meet Sunny – Jennie's big sister. Since I apologised to Jennie, she would slow down to say hi and remind me that I owe her a bike ride in October. She even asked if I were able to find the Abus lock online. When I hear the bicycle bell, I turn to greet Jennie only to find myself being stared down by a very fierce-looking Chinese girl on a black bike. Her hair is much darker than Jennie's, but they have the same colour eyes, only Sunny's are not very friendly.

"You are David. Yes? You listen to me real good, Little Boy. You make Jennie cry again I will take my tiger sword and fillet you from gullet to gut. You hear me, Boy. I told Jennie not to talk to you. Some hero you turned out to be. I'm watching you." And off she goes, leaving me with no doubt in my mind that she meant every single word she said. My heart is still racing when I reach home in a hurry. I keep imagining Sunny popping out from behind a hedge or a tree brandishing her tiger sword.

At four, Adam rings the bell. When he sees me, he shakes his head: "We are not going to park today are we? You walk home every day from school, why do you get so stiff? Don't you do any exercise…?" Adam stops talking when he sees me counting on my fingers. "I forgot about the one-question rule. What must I do with the other questions?"

"You keep them in your head and ask them one by one. We do three blocks today so that my muscles can recuperate from the unusual torture yesterday."

"Muscles?"

"I have them, they are just undercover lately. Come summer, you will see my muscles."

Adam does not look convinced, but he wisely let it go. "If you walk home from school every day, why are you so stiff?"

"Different muscle groups. I'm bigger than you, my shoulders and arms also took a beating on those belly buttons of the Anaconda."

Adam grins. "You are going to need a lot of practice to get to three minutes and fifty-five seconds."

Strangely, Adam keeps pace with me for the three-block ride and does not race ahead as–usual. He is also quiet, but I do not really notice as I am looking out for a Chinese girl with a tiger sword.

"Why are you looking over your shoulder so much? "

"Just looking, you know. Dogs."

That makes Adam laugh a big belly laugh. He keeps smiling all the way home. When we got home, he asks me the same question he asks every time day: "Will I see you tomorrow?"

"Yes, you only need to ring the bell, I'll come down. See you tomorrow."

After dinner, which does not include any peas, only the sweet-tasting beeshart tomato in a green salad, Dad says he wants to talk to me. While doing the dishes, I try to figure out what I did wrong. The only other, and even worse, possibility is that Mom scheduled the meeting with Big Henry and the wild dogs' parents. For once, Perfect Amelia did not have a go at me, and that makes me even more nervous. She was quiet through dinner also.

When I show up to face the music, Mom is also there. This is super bad.

Dad is sitting in front of his laptop. "Davey, your mom, and I have been looking at your school's community event calendar..."

Crap, did Dad find out that it is a fake calendar? My stomach starts to hurt again.

"Davey, answer your dad. Do you not think it is a good opportunity for all of us to discuss the bullying at school?"

I really need to listen and not let my mind wander off into dark corners when Dad is talking. I do not like the 'all of us' idea. "Mom, I want to do this alone."

"But Love, do you not think it would be better if Dad and I also speak up at the meeting? You know, as parents."

Dad is still staring at his laptop as if he could find the answer there. When he looks up, the white screen reflects in his glasses. I cannot see his eyes. "Why do you want to do this alone, Davey?"

Because it is not a real event. I could not possibly tell Dad that.

"I... I... You always interfere when Big Henry and the others bully me." Hell, that came out wrong, by the look on Dad's face, it does not go down too well either. "That's not what I mean – I mean you and Mom always help, you always come to save me and talk to the principal, but you are not with me the whole day – every day. I need to do this by myself; I must stand up for myself. Like I did the other day when I got detention." Sherbet, should not have said that either.

"Davey, when did you get detention? You did not say anything about detention. When did this happen? Where is the slip for me to sign?" Luckily, Mom is asking the questions before Dad could get in a word.

This hole is getting deeper and deeper. "Two weeks ago."

"Two weeks. And you did not say a word!" Mom's voice is going higher and higher. "You lied to us – when did you sit detention? This is so unlike you. Why are you doing this?"

"Bubbles, give the boy a chance to talk." Dad gently puts his arm around Mom to quiet her down, but his look promises retribution. You do not upset his wife without consequences. "Please explain, David."

"I did not do it on purpose. It just happened. Big Henry and his wild… friends were poking me with their fingers, when I shoved at Peter to get him to stop, he fell down. Mr Potgieter saw that. He said I was the hooligan. He let Big Henry go without giving him a warning, but now I'm sitting detention for four weeks. I did not get a slip. I did not know about the slip, it is my first time. I'll ask tomorrow. Promise."

The silence stretches on and on. I look at my feet, the pictures on the wall, the laptop on Dad's desk. Anywhere but a Mom and Dad.

"Do you plan to make this a regular occurrence?" Dad sounds so reasonable; it is scary.

"No... no Dad." I dare to take a peek at Dad. He does not look upset, he seems... blank. Perfect Amelia calls that look his German face. Mom, on the other hand, looks between crying and disbelieve.

"Davey, Love....what. You never get into fights. What is going on?"

"Mom, I swear..."

"David..."

In our house, you do not swear. It is a religious thing, because when you swear you call God as a witness. You cannot call God to witness frivolous things. It is up there with taking God's name in vain; instead, we promise; we give our word; we guarantee, but we do not swear.

"I promise I did not do it on purpose. It just happened. I did not know that Peter would fall; he is so much bigger and taller than me. Really, I promise. It was not really a fight, I just wanted him to stop poking me in the stomach with his fingers, you know."

Mom gives a tired sigh "Hank, you deal with this. You are better equipped." Leaving Dad and me staring at her back.

Dad looks at me, and I look at Dad. What now? Dad runs his fingers through his brush cut. "You need a haircut, Davey."

Ok, not what I expected. "Yes, Dad."

"My wife, your mother, by the grace of God, is distraught because of your actions. You shall apologise to my wife. I do not condone your behaviour, but I do understand that the circumstances made you act without thought. I want to say that this is your one and only warning, but I do suspect that we will have this conversation several times in the future. I shall deal with each transgression on its own merit. There shall be no electronic media for you for a whole week. You shall also clean the yard each Saturday for four weeks without help. And you shall do the dishes on your own for the next two weeks. Do you understand?"

"Yes, Dad." I begin to breathe again.

"Go and make your mom a cup of tea, she is quite upset with your behaviour." I was halfway out the door when Dad drops the bomb.

"David, you shall prepare a speech to present at the bullying event at school. You shall also report back on what you have learned. I want to see your speech three days before the event so that we could work on your presentation."

I have just hit the centre of the earth. My guardian angel must be laughing his ass off. Lying never pays. I make tea for Mom and also a cup for Amelia for good measure.

Mom smiles when I tortoise walks into her workroom with a full teacup in a saucer. "Still my Davey."

When I take Amelia her tea, I can see that she has been crying. I do not know what to say to her. I just pat her shoulder and get out of there as fast as I can. Perhaps I should tell Mom, but as Mom has already been upset once this evening, I'm keeping my fingers crossed that this will sort it out by itself. Boy, was I wrong!

Year 1; Month 3; Week 11

Captain David Zacharias Log
Stardate 71178.2. Log Entry 124. Week 11.

Adam is sick.

The week started out good with Mom making our new favourite oatmeal breakfast with the toasted almonds and honey yoghurt. Even my lunchbox looked super delicious, with a homemade pistachio chocolate bar, apple slices, and a rye sandwich with cheese, beeshart tomato, and basil. For one perfect moment in time, life seemed good and then it all went down the drain.

The first period on Wednesday, I had a run-in with Big Henry and the wild dogs. They held me down and wrote *Little Nuke* in purple marker on my white shirt. I had to go to the office to find an old jersey to wear the whole day.

The second period was uneventful. If getting fifty-two percent on an English literacy test can be considered as a non-event in the grand scheme of things.

Third period I fell down the stairs when Peter paid me back for shoving him two weeks ago.

Fourth period Ms Daniels makes me stand in front of the class with three other kids to explain body shapes. I am an apple, if you are wondering.

During first break, I lost my jersey when Big Henry got hold of it, and half the kids on the playground saw my big white whale stomach when he shook me out of it. The pear-shaped girl later gave it back to me. The rest of the day followed the same pattern of torture and bad marks, but what hurt the most of all was when Jennie did not even say 'hi' when we ran into each other seventh period on the stairs. I keep hoping it was because she was with her friends and did not want to talk to me in front of them.

When four rolls around, I'm happy to see Adam and his big smile. "Hi, Adam, ready for the park today?"

"Yes, I'm always ready for the park. You gonna practice for Friday? There are lots of seconds between four minutes and one second and three minutes and fifty-five seconds. A whole six seconds. You will have to jump all the belly buttons and maybe even some of the humps. Perhaps you could make up time on the fangs you have good balance."

"You do know that snakes do not have belly buttons. They come from eggs; they do not need belly buttons."

"This Anaconda is a mutant. It has belly buttons, lots of them." Adam does not care; in his fantasy world, snakes have belly buttons. At the park, Adam gets off his bike and sits down on a boulder.

"You are not going to ride the Anaconda today?"

He gives me a bright smile: "No. I'll be your coach. You need to practice to get rid of those six seconds. It is not as easy as you think. I'll keep time." This is strange; usually, Adam will race ahead and I'll try my best to catch up. "Say 'go' so that I know when to press the button."

I give him another look, but Adam seems happy to play coach. I yell 'go' and charge down the fangs twisting and turning, miss the first belly button, wobble over the second, jump the third and chicken out on the stair jump and finally made it safely to the end. Completely out of breath, I push the bike to where Adam is sitting. "What's the time?"

"It bad, see for yourself." I did not look at the time – I stare in shock at Adam's hands. His knuckles are all red and swollen, even his wrist bones are red. He could barely hold onto the watch. "Four minutes and eight seconds. You are slower than last time. Go again. This time do not look at your front wheel. You have to look further ahead, then you can see what part of the snake is coming."

I want to ask him about his hands, but Adam is pretending that nothing is wrong. I bike to the head of the snake and yell, "Go!"

"You are not looking, Slim, look ahead. Belly coming up. Go faster for the jump. Yeah, you did it, watch out for the ribs." Adam keeps yelling instructions and encouragements. I just keep going through the motions; inside I'm scared and cold.

"You did it, Slim! Look, Davey. Four minutes zero seconds. You're fastest yet. Come on, one more time."

"Hey! My legs feel like jelly; let me rest up, then I'll go again. Where is the water?"

I sit down next to Adam. He gives me the water and continues to instruct me on how to race faster. I do not hear a single word. The only words going round and round in my head are: "Adam is sick. Adam is sick."

I again run the Anaconda twice. My best time, three minutes and fifty-eight seconds. It is difficult to smile and joke with Adam as if nothing is wrong.

"See you are doing so well because I'm an excellent coach. With my help, you will go much faster than three minutes and fifty-five seconds. I bet you could go to fifty seconds. Just like that." On the way home, he keeps on talking and joking but does not race ahead as usual. His talk about his excellent skills as a coach finally drills through the fog in my head and gives me an idea.

"Adam, I will not be able to go biking tomorrow afternoon. I have to study."

"Ok." I am surprised when he does not ask any questions. His silence unnerves me, I want to talk to chase away the quiet. "It is a language test. I got horrible marks on the last test. When Mom sees it, she will most probably send me to language lessons three times a week."

"What language are you learning?"

"English."

That gets his attention. "English? You are speaking English already. Why must you learn it? Is English your second language? What were your marks? Do you speak German at home? Say something in German." Adam is looking me up and down like I have turned into an alien or something.

"I speak English, but when I write in English, I get confused between the verbs, the adverbs, nouns, pronouns, prepositions, etcetera, etcetera. Because I know that I'm confusing them, I will choose my second answer, but the first one is right, then I change it again… and that is how you score fifty-two for an English language test."

Adam finds it hilarious and cannot stop giggling. "You nearly failed! What are you going to do?"

"I do not know. You are an excellent coach, so you tell me." I do not have to try too hard to sound grumpy in the face of his apparent joy about my lack of language skills.

"I know – you must make up a rhyme to remember which one is which. I'll help you. I know what a verb is. Verb is the name of Herbert's workhorse. See? It is easy. A verb does the work; it is an action word. I also know one for a noun. Noun is the name of the game. Miss Emmy says that proper nouns have capital letters because the Queen of England speaks proper English, but the common people do not. See easy. Now you already know a lot of English language."

"Ok, Coach, since you know your nouns give me one for an adjective."

"I know that one too. An adjective is a superhero's secret weapon. Do you know what the adjectives are in that sentence?" I notice that while Adam is happily giving language lessons, he is very pale with two bright red spots on his cheeks. How did I miss it this afternoon? Once again, I was so self-absorbed that I did not even once get out of my own head to look at Adam and really see him.

"I'll have to guess, super, and secret."

"I told you I'm good. What else do you have to learn? I can make more rhymes for you." We are at the gate, but I can see that Adam does not want to go home. He just stands there and makes no move to open the gate. "Will I see you on Friday?"

"No, I'm going to be late." I can see the light going out of Adam. His shoulders slump, and he becomes this lost, lonely kid. In an exaggerated whisper, I tell him. "I'm sitting detention. Do not tell anybody."

His eyes grow big in his head his mouth a perfect O. He whispers back: "What did you do?"

Keeping an eye out for Ms McKenzie, I whisper: "I got in a fight." And then louder. "I'll see you tomorrow for some more language lessons. Hello, Ms McKenzie, we are on time today."

Adam's Mom gives me a tired smile. "Hi, Davey. How are you? Did the practice go well?"

"Mommy, Davey ran the Anaconda in three minutes and fifty-eight seconds. I'm his coach. I'm training him."

"That nice, Adam. Let's go, Davey still has homework to do."

I watch him leave. At the door, he stops and turns back.

"Are you still coming tomorrow? I know lots of rhymes for English. I can even think up new ones. I promise I can help you study. Please."

"No worries, Coach, I'll be there."

Once through the gate, I could not get off my bike fast enough. I left it against the garage and go looking for Mom. "Mom, Mom!"

"Davey, what is wrong?" Mom's hands are still dripping water when she grabs hold of my arms. "Are you hurt?"

"No, Mom. Adam is sick. You must see his hands; they are all red and swollen, he is pale and did not even race me today. He just wanted to sit down and watch me run the Anaconda. Mom, what is going to happen? Is he going to die? Is it my fault because we were late on Monday? I'm scared Mom. I do not want him to die." I don't know why I'm crying – I'm not sick."

Mom pulls me in a close hug. "It is ok, Davey. Megan called, she knows Adam is having an episode, but he very much wanted to go with you to the park, so she let him go today. Adam cannot go out again for the next week or two. He is going to be ok. He is so much stronger than he was. You can see him again later."

"No. I'm going to see him tomorrow." I pulled away from Mom's hug so that I can see her face.

"No, Davey. It is better if you do not disturb him when he is sick." Mom wipes my tears away with the palm of her hands.

"I shake my head and push her hands away. " No. I'm going to see him tomorrow. I promised him. I'm not going to be like his father who runs away because Adam is ill. I promised him. He is going to help me study."

"Davey, it is not that simple. He needs to rest and stay away from people so that his immune system can get strong again. He will understand."

I'm not going to let it go. "No, Adam made me promise to come tomorrow. You can ask his mom, she was there. I promised him, Mom. What if I bathe before I go, then I'll be really clean and… and I'll wear a facemask as they did in that medical series on TV. Please, Mom, talk to Adam's mom. Please-please." Now I was scared that I would let Adam down. I can still see his face when I told him that I was not seeing him on Thursday.

"Please, Mom" I search for her cell phone and put it in her hand. "Please call Ms McKenzie. She will tell you I told him that I'll see him tomorrow. Dad says your word is your bond. I'm not going to break my word." I'm shaking all over.

"Calm down, Davey. I'll call her later." She puts her hand over my mouth when I start to protest again. "Davey, she is busy getting Adam ready for bed. I'll call her at eight. I promise. Now calm down. Go wash your face. Then put your bike in the garage." Mom pushes me out the door and watches me go up the stairs. At the landing, I turn to check again. "I promise to call at eight. Go now."

When I put my bike away, I keep looking at his window – perhaps Adam will see me in the garage house, but I can see no shadows in the lighted window. I hope he is going to be ok. I want him to be ok. He is my friend. My only real friend.

All through dinner, I keep watching the time, hoping that, if I look up, it is eight o clock and time for Mom to call. The time drags by. I do not even know what we are eating. I rush through stacking the dishes and wiping the counters. When Mom says I'm done, I fly up the stairs. I have an idea to make Adam feel better and convince him that I'll be there tomorrow. I want to send him an e-mail, but since my electronic privileges are suspended, I need Perfect Amelia's help. Her door is open. She is busy studying, the laptop open on a math problem. I knock on the open door and wait for her to notice me. "Amelia, can you send an e-mail to Adam for me? Please."

"You know you are not supposed to use the internet." The look on my face must have convinced her that this is serious. "Show me what you want me to send to him."

I show her my English test with the 52% score. "You want me to e-mail Adam you're close to failing test results? Whatever for?" She is holding onto the test paper as if it is something that needs to be disposed of. Disgust clearly evident on her face.

"Adam says he will help me to get better marks in my next test. He seems to know all the rules and stuff. Please, just take a picture of it and e-mail it to Adam so that he can see that I need his help. Here is his address. Please, Amelia, I need to make sure that Adam knows I'm not going to disappear on him because he's sick."

"What do you want me to say?"

"Just put 70% in the subject line and says it comes from me."

Amelia does not say anything, just smooths out the paper and takes the picture, she uploads the file from her WhatsApp, and e-mail it to Adam. "Here. I have done what you asked. Has Mom said you can go tomorrow?"

"Not yet, I have to wait until eight when Mom is going to call. I just have to wait another 28 minutes. Thanks for helping."

"Mmm, let me know what Mom says." Amelia turns back to her homework.

Just past eight, Amelia joins me at the top of the stairs while Mom speaks to Ms McKenzie. It feels like forever, but it is only about fifteen minutes when Mom stops at the bottom and gives me the thumbs-up sign.

"You are cleared to visit. But, Davey, you must not tire him out – only an hour. Same time you usually go biking. Ok?"

"Yes, Mom, I promise. How is Adam?"

"He has a high fever and is in pain, but he is going to be ok. Megan also says thank you for Amelia's e-mail." Mom looks at Amelia, waiting for an explanation, but Dad calls to Mom, and we are saved from answering.

There is still light in Adam's bedroom when I get ready for bed, so I put my night light in the window in case Adam looks out, he'll understand that I'm thinking about him and he is not alone. I do not want him to feel alone.

The next day, it feels like school is dragging on and on. I'm sure time has slowed down. I barely notice the teasing and the poking. For the first time, I realise the effect that Dad's punishment of no electronic communication is having on my life. I want to check on Adam but have no cell phone; the payphone in front of the office was removed a few years ago when cell phones were allowed for emergency calls. When the last bell rings for the day, I cannot get out of the classroom fast enough.

I am well into my second block on the way home when Big Henry and the wild dogs catch up with me.

"Where's the fire, Little Nuke?" Pieter smacks me between the shoulders, I stumble forward, nearly kissing the pavement. "Ow, so sorry, Nuke, just happy to see you. Where are you off to in such a rush?"

"Maybe his mommy is waiting for him." Big Henry once again pulls me into his sweaty armpit and keeps pace with me.

"No, I need to get home. My friend is sick."

"You have a friend we do not know about, Little Nuke? That's not right." Big Henry sounds genuinely upset. "Are we not friends? Will you come running if one of us is hurt? You know rugby is a dangerous sport. Look at the bruise on Crunch's arm. You did not even ask him if he is hurt. Shame on you, Little Nuke, we greet you every day, and you are not concerned about our health." He pulls me to a stop. "Ask him nicely, Little Nuke," and Big Henry waves in the direction of the Crunch who is looking at me with a pained expression in his eyes.

"How is your arm, Crunch?" Going along with their game might get them off my back quickly.

Big Henry shakes me, my head whipping back and forth, and my teeth clattering together. My bubble gum flies out of my mouth, missing the Crunch by millimeters, and smacks into Peter who is standing behind him. Big Henry finds it hilarious but Peter not so much. He elbows Crunch out of the way and grabs my shirt:

"You did that on purpose – you fat blob." His spit baths my face. Peter hits me with his fist in the stomach, I stumble backwards into Big Henry, who is still holding onto me. Pain explodes in my stomach, my breath locks in my throat. My vision blurs. I feel nauseous, sweat beading on my forehead. For a second I hang limply in Big Henry's arms.

"Hey, watch out, you stupid ape."

A car hoots and big Henry shoves me in the direction of the sidewalk. I stumble, black spots dancing in front of me. I struggle to breathe. My stomach hurts – a burning pulsing fire. The car slows to a stop, and the window rolls down to reveal Mr Potgieter glaring at me of all people.

"Mr Miller, it seems trouble always finds you. Should you not wish to extend your stay in detention with another two weeks, I suggest you be on your way. Henry, you really must be more careful. Can't have our star player injured before the big game."

While Mr Potgieter enquires about the rugby players' health, I make my escape cradling my painful stomach all the way home. Of course, at home, I run straight into Perfect Amelia. "You home early. What happened to you? Tuck in your shirt. Do you not have any pride?" She looks me up and down. "You were in another fight. How long do you want to be offline?" But she did not blab on me.

I wince at the stinging pain when I push in my shirt and quickly fasten the top buttons before I go looking for Mom. "Mom...Mom, I'm home. Is Adam ok? Did Ms McKenzie call?"

"Slow down, Davey. Adam is fine. He still has a fever, but he is fine. You can go and see him at four." Finally having some news makes me feel like a weight has been lifted that I did not even know I was carrying. The knot in my stomach loosens up. I'm so happy about Adam that I do not complain about the tuna salad and English muffins for lunch. Mom added Danish Feta, it is smooth and creamy on my tongue. Even my upset stomach does not complain about this delight. "Thanks, Mom – this is nice."

Around three o'clock, I give up. I could not concentrate on my homework. I want to see for myself that Adam is ok. His swollen, red hands haunt me. I decide to take a quick shower. Being clean could do no harm. I dress in my favourite grey and red long-sleeve T-shirt and my good denim jeans. When I stuck my hands in the pockets, the jeans slide lower down on my hips. My underpants poke their nose out to the world. This would not do at all. I do not want Ms McKenzie to think I'm some gangsta dude. I need a belt or one denim in a smaller size. I did not even realise that I have lost this much weight. It is an unexpected surprise, but somehow the happiness that should go with the realisation is not there. I find a belt but now the denim bulges in the front. I need to find a smaller size. A quick search and I pull out jeans with a tear on the knee, but at least it covers my underpants.

Finally, it is time to go see Adam. Armed with my notebook and pen, I rush down the stairs, shouting at Mom that I'm leaving. The door slams closed behind me. I'm going to pay for that later, but for now, I want to see Adam. When I ring the bell at the gate, a tired-looking Ms McKenzie opens the gate.

"Hi, Davey, I'm glad you came. Adam's upstairs. Go up. he's been waiting the whole day."

"Thanks, Ms McKenzie."

I rush past her up the stairs. When I push open the door, I walk into a sick room. Adam's toy-filled room has been turned into a sterile room with plastic sheeting, drip stand, and medication everywhere. Even his bed has been raised so that his mom need not bend down to check on him. At this height, he can see right into our backyard. Adam is sitting up watching the door, laptop ready for our language lesson.

"Hi there. How are you doing?"

His cheeks are red, his hair is damp from the fever. Adam's hands are even more swollen than yesterday. He looks tired but determined.

"I'm good. You really messed up that test. Why did Amelia send me the email? Who did you fight with? Did you hit him? What did… ?"

I shush him with my finger when I hear his mum coming up the stairs. It will not make a good impression if she knows I have gotten into a fight and have to sit detention.

"Adam, give Davey a chance to sit down before you grill him. Would you like something to drink? Coke? Anything to eat?"

"I'm all good, thanks, Ms McKenzie."

She pulls a chair from the desk and places it close to the bed. "Here you go. Call me if you need anything. I'll be downstairs. Adam, remember Davey is here to study not play. Ok?" Her usually neat hair has fallen from her bun, and if I am not mistaken, her blouse is buttoned up all wrong. His mom has barely closed the door when Adam starts with the questions again.

In order to get any work done, I tell Adam about the non-fight that resulted in my detention and me being off-line for two weeks as punishment." He wants to know everything and keep asking until satisfied with the retelling.

"Not even telephone?"

"Nada. Nothing. No electronics at all. I had to ask Perfect Amelia to send you an e-mail. Did not want to push my luck to try and ask her if I could borrow her cell phone to call you."

"Why are you bullied at school? It is because you are fat? Will it stop when you are no longer fat?

"I do not know. Could we talk about this later? I'm more stressed about failing the Language test tomorrow, as it counts towards my exam. I do need to get better marks."

Finally, we could get to work. Adam has been busy, he has printed out my test, and in neat round letters wrote out all the correct answers and the rhymes that go with them. He has pulled tests from the web and patiently explains when I give the wrong answer. This is so unlike the Adam who is always in a rush to get somewhere and get things done.

It is only when the room is getting dark that I realise that more than an hour has passed. It is closer to six. Strange that Adam's Mom has not yet come up to tell me that my time is up. I just hope that she does not know about my bad marks and thought I need more than an hour to get it right. I say a quick goodbye to Adam and promise to see him tomorrow. He must have been tired, as he did not protest at all.

Just as I walk out of the room, he speaks again. "Hey, Slim, thanks for putting the light in the window. I looked at it all night."

I quietly slip down the stairs, thinking that I could leave without Ms McKenzie knowing that I kept Adam busy so late. But I forgot that she needs to open the electronic gate for me. I found her sleeping on her arms on her desk, paperwork everywhere. Now I know why the usually neat Adam's room looks like a disaster zone. What must I do now? I do not want to wake her, but I cannot see the remote anywhere. I retraced my steps to the bottom of the stairs and call out to Ms McKenzie. I pretend to be busy reading in my notebook when she steps through the door. Her watch has made a groove on a cheek, her hair is even messier than before. She looks flustered and embarrassed.

"Look at the time, goodness. I did not even notice. You ready for your test tomorrow?"

"I think so, Adam made sure that I score 83% on a dummy test before he said I'm ready. He is a hard taskmaster. Thanks for letting me study with him."

At the gate, she gives me a surprise hug: "You are a good friend, Davey. Will we see you tomorrow?"

"Definitely – I have to return the favour – going to help Adam with his maths."

At dinner, the talk is all about Adam. I ask Mom if she could perhaps make some food that I can take with me on Friday because Adam's mom is so tired. Mom says she will make Jamie's tikka chicken dish, as Adam is on a special diet. I did not know that. He may not eat refined food like white bread and cookies and also red meat and lots of other foods. The tikka chicken dish would be perfect.

On Friday, Ms McKenzie is so surprised and happy when I give her the covered tikka chicken dish. I do what Amelia suggested and pretend that I feel terrible about overstaying on Thursday and the tikka chicken is an apology. She happily accepts that.

Adam's first words are about the language test. I give him a copy of the questions. When we worked through the answers it seems that I may score in the 70's – Adam says I only messed up four times, but I could not remember all of the answers, so there might be some more mistakes. We make a good study team. I only stay for an hour and promise to visit over the weekend.

When I pop in on Saturday, after my punishment yard work is done, I find a very grumpy and frustrated Adam. He even shouts at his mom, bursts out in tears, and makes me wish that I had not shown up for a visit. After a rather hasty exit, I get a brainwave. We have quite a long driveway with two gates. I decide to build my own obstacle course to practice for the Anaconda. I go looking for Mom and explain to her that Adam is very bored and frustrated. I think I can help by riding my bike up and down the driveway where Adam can see me and time my progress. Mom is busy with some church stuff for the choir and just nods her head and waves me out of the way.

I use the stuff from the garage to build my mini-Anaconda. We even have four orange cones that I spaced out with some crates in between. Three black car mats folded in half become belly buttons. Once, while I was riding in the garage, I crashed into a box which fell over, and this strange thick carpet made of wood blocks and rope fell out.

I now push and pull the massive thing halfway down the driveway to create a rough surface like the one in the park. After all that pushing and pulling, I was so tired I lay down for a rest, but a rubber ball bouncing down the driveway quickly make me sit up. What on earth? A second ball followed the first, barely missing me. I look up in shock. Adam is the one throwing rubber balls at me! He's waving at me from his bedroom window. How did he get out of bed with the drip attached? . Great, his mom is going to kill me. He must have realised the same thing as he quickly closes the window and disappears from view.

I drag my tired body upright and wish I never started this project in the first place, put on my helmet, gloves and knee guards and get on my bike. I tap my wrist to let Adam know to time me, take a deep breath and charge down the mini-Anaconda. I find the twist and turns thought the orange cones easy, but the boxes and crates are bigger and broader, and I have to stop twice to rebalance before going on. I clear the first two jumps with ease, misjudged the box and the distance to the next jump, and ended up against the wall. Thank Heavens for my gloves and knee guards else, I would have been picking my skin from the wall. I wobble all over the woodblock mat but managed to stay upright until the end. Somehow the mini-Anaconda tuned out more complicated than it looks.

"You were watching your front wheel, that is why you misjudged the distance." Perfect Amelia's sudden appearance manages to do what the obstacle course could not do…. flat on my ass on the ground. What the hell! When I look up, Amelia is studying me with a pitiful expression. "Your time is three minutes twenty-two seconds; compared to the distance you covered, it is beyond slow." Then she turns around and saunters to the top of the drive where she takes a seat on one of the planters. "Get on with it; I do not have all day."

It seems the fall must have damaged my hearing. "What do you mean, get on with it? Why are you sitting there? Why are you even home, are you not supposed to be out with Barney?"

Amelia flicks her long blond hair back and looks down her nose at me. "Do you want to know what Adam is texting or not?" I look up at his bedroom window, but there is no sign of him. At the same time, Amelia's phone beeps again. "Adam says you have rested long enough, try again, this time look ahead." She waves me in the direction of the mini-Anaconda.

"Are you just going to sit there?"

"No, I'm going to relay Adam's messages out of the goodness of my heart. It is not as if I can run up and down the stairs the whole time."

"You can leave your phone here and go do your stuff – you do not need to watch me all the time." She is making me nervous; I do not need an audience.

"And get in trouble with Dad. No, thank you. Davey, just go ride your bike down that thing you built. Adam is waiting." And right on cue, her phone beeps again. I do not wait around to hear the message and take off for the starting point. I concentrate on getting over and around the obstacles, making sure that I look further ahead than my front wheel. Ignoring Amelia's presence as best as I can. When I reach the end, I breathe a sigh of relief and wipe the sweat from my face.

"Three minutes and 12 seconds, you are getting better at this. Do it again – you can get your time down to three minutes." Amelia is now totally invested in my performance; she walks down the course, aligning boxes and crates, kicking stones and leaves out of the way. She looks like an inspector, only needing the clipboard. She is eye-balling me expectantly "Are you ready?"

"No, I'm thirsty. I going to get water. You want some." I've taken off my helmet to let the breeze cool me down. This is hard work.

"Yes – thanks." Amelia is refolding the rubber mat, not worried at all that she is dirtying her hands.

Coming back from the kitchen with two glasses, I'm stopped in my tracks at sight never seen before in my eleven soon to be twelve years on earth. My perfect, always in control, super composed and elegant sister is attempting the mini-Anaconda on her fuchsia pink bike. It is a spectacle to behold and remember in the years to come. She's holding her own around the cones and the boxes but lacks the strength to jump the rolled-up mats. Her front wheel would hit the mat and come to a shuddering stop. She has to quickly drop her feet to keep the bike upright. Since Perfect Amelia is my dad's daughter, she does not give up. Backing up, she tries again. Again, she hits the mat and comes to a standstill.

"Stand up, you will have more power and pull up on the handles." She backs up; the back wheel hits the crate and moves it out of the way. She bends down and pulls the crate back to its original position.

"Leave it, the extra space would allow you more speed." For my trouble, I get a dirty look.

"I can do this." This time she stands up on the pedals. Aggravation lends her strength, the front of the bike clears the mat, but the back wheel comes down behind it, leaving her stuck. I can hear her groan with frustration. "This is so much harder than it looks." She takes a deep breath; resolve written all over her face, and with a hop, she is over the mat.

104

I now take up the position on the planter, wisely keeping my comments to myself and watch the wondrous spectacle of Perfect Amelia taking on the mini-Anaconda. The woodblock mat is nearly her undoing. Being in a lighter weight class than me, the blocks roll away from her wheels, throwing her off balance and she came close to crashing. When I stand up to offer my help, a fierce glare sits me down again, but I could not keep the smirk from my face.

She joins me at the planter, her face red, sweat beading her forehead and breathing hard: "Where did you get this crazy plan from?" She pulls her helmet from her head, I can only stare at this new unkempt version of Perfect Amelia.

"Adam and I usually do the obstacle course at Rotary Park," I answer casually as if this is an everyday occurrence, not just twice. "Want to try again?"

"Yes, but you first." Her phone beeps. I just know it is Adam, and even though I desperately want to know what her time is, I'm not brave enough to ask.

It turned out to be a fun afternoon. Amelia has put her phone on speaker so that we could hear Adam's comments and instructions. We took turns riding the mini-Anaconda only stopping for the day when my legs turned to jelly, my shoulders and arms aching so much that I lack the strength to jump the bellies. I hit the two minutes and forty-eight seconds mark twice and Amelia's best time – three minutes and four seconds. I learned that my sister is funny, with a quirky sense of humour. She quickly catches onto Adam-speak topping him in crazy. No wonder she is so popular at school.

This is a week full of surprises. On Thursday, when I storm into Adam's room to hear my block cycling time, I run into a tall dark-haired man standing with his back to the door. I do not know who is the most surprised; he recovers first.

"I can see manners are not your strong point. Knocking before entering another person's personal space is an accepted custom and deems to be polite. Who are you?"

"Davey. David Miller. I live next door." I glance at Adam for help, but a very subdued and teary Adam is hunkering down in the bed. He appears small and lost, bullied into submission. A wave of anger gives me the courage to look the man full in the eye.

"I am Adam's friend. We usually go biking together, but Adam is taking a few sick days. He is also my English language tutor. I got eighty-three per cent on a test since Adam's started to help me."

He inspects me from my brush-cut head to dirty sneakers, his lips pulling an upside-down crescent moon – clearly not impressed by the overweight, language challenged boy from next door. "You look older than ten. How old are you?"

"I am eleven." The little devil on my shoulder makes me add: "Turning twelve in October."

"Did you fail a grade?" I can hear Adam's suppressed snicker, his sense of humour has not disappeared completely.

"No, Sir. I passed all my grades the first time. I am in grade six. Just subtract two if you want to know the standard." I catch sight of Adam's open mouth astonishment at my belligerence, then I realise that Adam and this man have the same curly mop of hair. Now both McKenzie men are staring at me for different reasons. I finally met Adam's dad – the always absent Advocate Ian McKenzie.

In for a penny, in for a pound, so I stoke the fires. "I'm here for Adam's maths lesson."

The advocate nearly chokes on his next breath with my statement. I will always wonder what he would have said if Ms McKenzie did not step in to defuse the situation. She takes him by the arm and tells her clueless husband that I'm a math whizz and is tutoring Adam. When she pulls him from the room, her eyes are sparkling, she winks at me. But Advocate Ian did not get where he is in life by being a pushover and was back shortly to supervise the tutoring session. His presence makes Adam so nervous that the poor kid's brain turns to mush – he gives all the wrong answers. I decide to cut the lesson short and get out of there to save Adam.

At home, I find Mom in the kitchen, getting dinner ready.

"I do not like Advocate Ian McKenzie either. He is a bully."

Before Mom could utter anything more than "David!" I ran up the stairs, my name sounding in my ears.

Year 1; Month 3; Week 12

Captain David Zacharias Log
Stardate 71197.4. Log Entry 12. Week 12.

Operation code name: White Whale.
1) Surviving my punishment – Asked Adam to help me with my bullying essay since he is so interested in the subject. And regret it later, he was very thorough in his research.
2) Keep Adam entertained. See number one. Can't wait for him to get better.
3) Losing weight – I now fit into last year's pants. A full size smaller.

.

Year 1; Month 3; Week 13

Captain David Zacharias Log
Stardate 71216.5. Log Entry 126. Week 13.

Operation code name: White Whale.
1) Punishment – Dad was happy with the essay. Called it well written. I did tell him Adam helped me out. He was not angry about it. My guardian angel seems to care since Dad did not ask about Community week.
2) Keep Adam entertained. I eventually figured out why Adam gets so grumpy. It seems the chaos in his usually neat room is driving him nuts. We tidied up his room, using all the sorting boxes left over when Mom put her foot down on the state of my room. Adam even made neat labels to sort out his medication so that his mom knows where to put what. Now that everything is put away in his cupboards, the only indication of him being ill is the drip stand next to the bed.
3) Losing weight – I'm a full pant size down. October is arriving too fast; I need to lose more weight before Jennie sees me on a bike.

Exams are about to start. Mom is cooking brain foods to make us smarter. Jamie, my hero to the rescue: yoghurt, cheese, green vegetables like beans and spinach, a leafy green power vegetable called kale (tastes like nothing), and worst of all, broccoli and Brussels sprouts. Also nutty brown rice, whole-wheat everything else; fish, lots of fish, blueberries; unsalted nuts; sunflower and pumpkin seeds, tomatoes and sweet potatoes. Do not forget the beans – I never knew there were that many. I do not like the mushy white beans; the red and black ones are nice. Fortunately, for me, it seems that peas do not make the cut for brain foods. But that does not stop the witch from bringing them to our doorstep, as for fruits – oranges and bananas. It turns out that, for exams, a banana is better than an apple since it calms the nerves. Oh, and do not forget the water – lots of water. A well-hydrated brain increases your cognitive ability.

My mom, who only wanted to know about sugar cereals and Cola a mere ten weeks ago, is now telling friends to eat the good foodstuff. I overheard her telling a lady friend at church that five servings of fruits and veggies are helping her losing weight without trying. She does not even exercise. Yes, we are turning into quite a healthy family, Mr Spock would be proud. He has once said: *"Change is the essential process of all existence."* When I heard Mr Spock say that the first time, it made me kind of sad. I do not want things to change; I was happy at that moment. Now it seems it is a positive way of thinking – change is good. Look at me – I'm losing weight and made a friend.

Year 1; Month 3; Week 14

Captain David Zacharias Log
Stardate 71235.7 Log Entry 127 Week 14.

Operation code name White whale
1) I served out my punishment – no more detention and finally got my phone and laptop back. Still doing yard work (healthy exercise).
2) Keep Adam, entertained. He is getting better and is off the drip and more mobile, which is now driving his Mom up the wall, as it seems she cannot keep him in bed. She threatens to tie him to it if she catches him outside again, but that has not happened yet.
3) Weight loss appears to be slowing down. Amelia says it is bound to happen, with all the stress of the exams and Adam's illness. I must just wait it out. My body will adjust. I really hope so as I'm not cheating or anything and I keeping up with the exercises.

Year 1; Month 3; Week 15

Captain David Zacharias Log
Stardate 71254.9. Log Entry 128. Week 15.

Operation code name: White Whale.
1) Exams have started with maths, algebra, and biology.
2) Adam is officially up and ready to take on the world. We did a slow lap around the block with his mom watching us. No Anaconda run yet.
3) Weight loss – too worried about the exams and the birthday party that just does not want to go away.

Two weeks. That's how long it takes for Adam to be up and about, and we could finally go biking again. The first few days we just go around the block, but by the end of the week, I'm left behind when Adam races down the sidewalks to the park.

Today we are back to our practice programme for St Michaels. Adam and I started our program on Easy Hill number one. In real life – Mossie Street. He is not impressed with my slow progress up the hill, mostly since he was the one that was on sick leave. Said that I'm wheezing like an old man, but I showed him a thing or two going downhill. First time I won Mister Speedy Adam in a race.

He got his own back, the next day I fell off my bike going downhill. Adam laughed so hard he also lost his balance and hit the ground. Another round of scolding about responsibility and safety from my mom but Adam's Mom did not look so stressed out. She did not scold us at all and was smiling at Adam's description of my ungainly head over ass fall off the bike. Fat kid on bike show right there in public.

Year 1; Month 4; Week 16

Captain David Zacharias Log
Stardate 71274.1. Log Entry 129. Week 16.

Operation code name: Cemetery Run
1) Avoid going down St Michaels as long as possible.
That is a killer mountain of a hill.
2) The second week of exams. English language; mathematics; geography; science.
3) Try to convince Mom that a birthday party is not necessary – no luck yet
4) Weight loss – too tired and stressed to care about my weight, but I do not cheat. Mom is now totally into Jamie Oliver, we are eating fresh fruit and vegetables every day. Dad also got with the program. On Saturday he made a roasted vegetable dish on the barbeque. Whole baby carrots; two different kinds of pumpkins; beetroot; tomatoes on the vine (that is when the tomatoes still have their green bits on) and small potatoes. Mom made a dessert with yoghurt, honey, and frozen fruits. Yummy! My lunchbox now has avocado and tomato on rye toast with a slice of soft white cheese. Amelia calls it ricotta – I'll take her word for it. I did not know you get orange and black tomatoes or even green ones. Quite delicious – thank you, Mr Oliver.

"Adam, please slow down; I cannot keep up with you. I'm sure you are drinking something to give you this much energy." Adam and I are timing our uphill and downhill battles, but it is a wasted effort, in my opinion. Mossie Street is beating me without any trouble.

"Common, Slim, you have been riding your bike the whole time I was in bed. You should be faster than this." I

117

can hear the frustration in his voice. The next moment he stops dead in his tracks. I have to swerve to miss him.

"Are you crazy, Adam Sullivan McKenzie? You do not just stop. I could have crashed into you. What's up with you today?" Adam has been cranky and snippy the whole afternoon.

He does not answer me, just takes his time, turning his bike around to face me, and then gets up real close and personal: "Are you doing this on purpose? Pretending to be tired so that I must slow down. Did Mommy put you up to this?" His dark eyes search my face, looking for an answer I do not have.

"What do you mean, doing it on purpose? I have been trying my best all week to go faster. And since when have you been telling your mom about our plans for St Michael. I thought this is all need to know, and the parents do not need to know." My temper is also flaring up. I do not need this on top of all the exam stress. Biking is supposed to be fun.

Adam is not letting go. "You are different. Always checking if I am ok. Stop doing that, you never did it before. Now you always asking: Are you alright, are you sure you are not tired. STOP ASKING! I'm always going to be sick; that is why it is called a chronic disease. I'm not going to die, stop worrying. Just be the old Davey. I'm not bugging you every day about losing weight." He is pounding on the handlebars in frustration.

That makes me remember my temper tantrum when Mom did not listen to me about wanting to lose weight. Then I realize I am behaving differently towards Adam – treating him like a sick person that needs to be taken care of. He is no longer Adam, the strange boy from next door. He is the sick kid. I have lost sight of Adam with his passion for life. He has enough people to tell him what to do and to take care because he is sick. He wants a friend to escape from all of it, to share his adventures and live a bit.

"Sorry, Adam. I am just worried about you. Believe me, I not trying to slow you down. I'm exhausted because I'm not sleeping and I'm stressing out about the exams."

For a long time, he just stares at me, not saying a single word. When I could not take the silence any longer, I rack my brains for something to say, to fill the awkward silence, but he starts to speak again in typical Adam style.

"Why are you stressing? An exam is just a bunch of tests one after the other. Do you not write tests every week? Sometimes more than one test a week. You got eighty-two percent on your language test, and you are a math wizard. So what is the problem?"

"It is an exam, Adam. It is difficult. There are more subjects than just English language and maths."

"It's still a test, is it not? You told me that you got the same question in a previous history test, so how it is different? Same questions same answers."

As usual, Adam's logic left me without a counter-argument. "I give up. Could we please just go?"

Adam shakes his head and mutters loud enough for me to hear: "Just a hype to make you think it worse than a test."

Year 1; Month 5 Week 17

Captain David Zacharias Log
Stardate 71293.4. Log Entry 13. Week 17.

Operation code name: Cemetery Run
1) Still trying to delay going down St Michaels as long as possible. The final week of exams, or like Adam calls it, hyper test week. I still have three tests left and then it is holiday time! Jippieeee!
2) I'm trying my best to convince Mom that a birthday party is not necessary. Making no headway and to make it worse, Grandpa Heinz and Grandma Edith are paying us a visit. Operation Spring clean is in full force everywhere – even the freezer is getting unpacked, labelled, and re-stacked in a mysterious order. We were ordered to keep out of the freezer and the fridge. No one dares to touch the grocery cupboard under threat of death. I had to polish the Eating Bell to its full silver glory.
3) Weight loss – think my body is still adjusting but keeping steady at my current weight. I'm back into last year's jeans. My favourite blue T-shirt with the starburst does not creep up over my belly anymore.

Amelia's boyfriend cheated on her, so she dumped him. High drama as Dad calls it. Luckily, exams will be done soon, and school will be closed for the holidays. I hope that not seeing the ass-hat (not my word – Amelia used a cruder term, I'm sure of it) at school would make it easier for her. I avoid the house as the tears, the screaming, and the music is driving me up to the wall. All of Amelia's friends are forever coming over for moral support. I can't tell by the shrieks if it is good or bad. In between, they would compliment and congratulate Mom on her weight loss. They think she is super cool. I flee the kitchen and the house – much safer over at Adam. That many women in one place are scary. Even Dad stays on the stoep while they are there. When I come home, he disappears into the den.

We eat comfort food. Mom says Amelia needs to be comforted. Mom made a vegetable chilli dish with cheesy potatoes. She even put peanut butter in the stew. And cacao. I'm not sure this is healthy, but she swears it is one of Jamie Olivier's superfood recipes. I liked the chicken dish that Mom made on Wednesday it's called hit-'n'-run chicken. That was for sure healthy. It had tomatoes, onions, red and yellow peppers and chicken – all in one pot in the oven. No frying.

Year 1; Month 5; Week 18

Captain David Zacharias Log
Stardate 71312.6. Log Entry 131. Week 18.

Operation code name: Cemetery Run
1) The holidays are here – No school and no St Michaels.
2) Still working on Mom and the birthday party
3) Weight loss – it is the holidays – I do not care.

"I think we should graduate from the Big Easy and move to Amelia's."

I stare at Adam in confusion. The holidays are finally here. We are riding our bikes on a flat stretch of the street at the bottom end of hill two. "Adam, what are you talking about? Where is Amelia? I look around, ready to flee if Amelia is anywhere near us – I cannot take any more of the breakup drama.

"No man, I named the inclines."

I come to a dead stop. "The inclines?"

Adam also stops and pulls his bike around. He has an intense look on his face when he answers "Yes. I named the street inclines to indicate their unique character."

"Their what?" Sometimes, when I ask a question, Adam would get this look on his face, which makes me think that he wants to pat me on the head and go: there-there now. Adam has that exact look on his face now.

"Slim, each street is a project and needs a name like a military operation. Mossie Street is the Big Easy, Loerie Street is the Rockies, and number three is Amelia. It was named The Serpent, but I renamed it to Amelia. Because the uphill is going to be difficult, it is much longer and winding not straight like the other streets. It will take time to get to the top, you know. My blank look prompted him to continue with a sigh as deep as the ocean is wide. "Slim, Amelia just broke up with her boyfriend. Mommy says there are five stages of grief, it is going to take a long time for her to get over her breakup. There are five cross streets on Amelia. Uphill 4 is Hurricane and Uphill 5 is Buster as in Ball Buster."

"Adam, the streets have names!"

"You want to conquer Peonies Avenue, Milk Thistle, and Mossie Street?"

Conquer? Thinking about it like that kind of make sense. I surrender to Adam's idea of renaming the hills (no inclines for me).

"What about St Michael Avenue?" I ask Adam when we are riding our bikes again. "Did you rename it also? Death Valley, Hell Road...."

Adam shakes his head. "No way. St Michael is an Archangel. He's the big shot of the angels and the patron saint of soldiers and the police.

That evening I try to explain to Mom why I do not want a birthday party – it does not matter if it is a significant number as she keeps telling me.

"Mom, please. There is no one at school that I want to invite to a party. Last year they just came because of the food. There was nothing in the boxes they left as presents. It was all a big joke. Why can't we just have a family barbeque since Grandma Edith is here?" Then I played my trump card. "I do not think Amelia is in a mood for a party now that Barney's out of the picture. Perhaps we could ask Adam and Ms McKenzie over since there are not a lot of people. Pleeeeaase."

For the first time, it seems as if Mom is considering the idea of not having a party. "You still want a cake, though?

I have found this great recipe online for a hummingbird cake that is really easy to make. I can reduce the calories with less sugar and substitute maybe half the oil with yoghurt. You are going to love it!" Mom's eyes are sparkling, her hands are talking a mile a minute. I really do not want to be a drag, but a hummingbird cake sounds kind of fairy princess-like to me.

"What is in this cake besides the oil and maybe yoghurt and sugar?"

Mom starts to laugh and hugs me close. She knows me so well. "Do not worry honey it is not a girly cake. It is made with banana, pineapple, and nuts. We could make a lemon zest cream-cheese frosting or even pecan brittle. What would you like?"

I still need a bit of convincing but if it means no party…

"Sounds interesting. Where did this cake come from?"

"Jamaica, according to Jamie Olivier. Over there it is called the doctor-bird cake after the Jamaican national bird.

"Did they give the cake to sick people? I do not want Adam to think we baked a healthy cake because he is sick." I really wish this birthday is over and gone – it is stressing me out. I have still to deal with Jennie and the bike ride I promised. The only positive is that I have lost a visible amount of weight and can even lose more – if only I could skip out on the party Mom is so set upon.

"No, Davey." Mom is still smiling, all excited about the cake. "The Jamaicans call their red-billed streamertail hummingbird the doctor bird because of the way the bird uses its long beak to check the flowers. It reminds them of a doctor examining a patient." I have to take her word for it, as I have never seen a red-billed streamertail hummingbird before.

"So, we are going to have a hummingbird cake that is not girly and a braai for my birthday." I was so sure that I have it in the bag before Mom walks right over my hopes.

"I have to speak to your dad first since Grandma Edith is here for your birthday."

"If it is my birthday like you said, why does Grandma Edith then get to dictate what kind of party I can have for my birthday? It is just stupid!" When Mom's eyebrow starts to rise, I shut my mouth real quick and clench my fists in frustration. If only the grandparents were not coming to visit.

"Grandma Edith and Grandpa Heinz are travelling all the way from Germany specifically to be here for your birthday. Turning twelve is a big birthday." And here it comes… "You are now turning into a teenager. It is a big step in growing up, becoming a responsible adult."

Blah, Blah, Blah. I have to bite hard on my teeth, not to point out that I'm a boy and not a girl. According to science, boys are way behind in the growing up race. Some even say we only grow up when we reach thirty-two – that is still a long long way to go. I wonder what Adam's opinion on birthday number twelve is. I must ask him when I see him again.

"Do you understand, Davey?"

"Yes, Mom. Sorry, Mom." I keep looking at the floor to avoid her eyes.

"Davey, look at me when I'm talking to you…"

The next moment Amelia rushes into the kitchen, holding her cell phone away from her as if it is going to bite her. "Mom, it's him. I do not want to talk to him. What should I do?" Amelia pushes the phone into Mom's hands and steps away to hide around the corner. It seems Barney has finally done me a favour. While the next chapter in the breakup drama unfolds, I make my escape.

Year 1; Month 5; Week 19

Captain David Zacharias Log
Stardate 71331.8. Log Entry 132. Week 19.

Operation code name: Cemetery Run
1) St Michaels is on hold. Advocate Ian seems to have moved back in permanently. Lucky for me, he works long hours and when we do meet; he is usually on the phone. His first action as Father of the Year is to take his family on a week-long holiday. I pretended to be happy for Adam, but I know it is to get Adam away from the moron next door. It is strange to go biking without Adam. I've decided that we need a training schedule, a very long one for St Michaels.
2) The birthday party is now officially a braai. The McKenzie's are invited – guess Adam's dad is not going to be happy.
3) Weight loss – it is the holidays. I do not care – sort of. Mom is still keeping us on the straight and narrow, but sometimes I wonder if she is not cheating. How can doughnuts be a healthy snack! Mom turned Jamie's breakfast doughnuts into an afternoon snack. According to Mom, it all about the way they are cooked – she boiled them. Even Dad did not believe her – we all saw the golden crispy doughnuts before she covered them with dollops of black cherry sauce with streaky white yoghurt drizzle. A sprig of mint topped off a most delicious afternoon snack. I'm keeping my fingers crossed.

"Hi, Davey, wait for me. I want to go with you."
I'm on my way down to go biking when I run into Amelia. She has been out with her girlfriends and is looking

really pretty in a blue denim dress with yellow embroidered flowers down the front. Naturally, her shoes match her dress perfectly. Her blond hair neatly caught in a fishtail braid. Perfect Amelia.

"Why?" Suspicion makes me sound rude. What's she up to?

Undeterred to rushes past me. "Give me ten minutes to get ready. I'll meet you at the garage."

Eight minutes later she arrives, dressed fashionably perfect for bike riding: dark blue cut-off denim, pink candy stripe T-shirt, and trainers. I silently hold out the matching pink bike helmet. I feel dowdy in my faded denim and grey shirt.

"Why are you doing this?"

She smiles; her big blue eyes all innocence. "It was such fun when we did the mini-anaconda that I wanted to see the original in the park. You are going to the park, are you not?"

Putting it like that, I could not argue. That was one of the best Saturday afternoons I had in a long time. Taking on the Anaconda alone in the park made me seem such a loser that I decided to stick to training on the Big Easy, the Rockies, and the Amelia Serpent. I was planning to try the Hurricane today, but this seems like much more fun.

"Ok, but if you fall and get hurt it is our own fault." I try one more time to get her to back out.

"Deal, little brother. Show the way."

We made good time in the park. When Amelia sees the Anaconda, she looks like a kid on Christmas morning, vibrating with suppressed joy and energy. She immediately takes off, inspecting the course.

"This is the mat! That was so clever of you." Amelia is standing at the section that looks like golf and tennis balls covered in concrete. "You did a good job with the mini-Anaconda. What is your best time on this one?"

"Three minutes and fifty-eight seconds."

While Amelia is busy inspecting the Anaconda, I check out the park and come to a sudden realisation, that in the holidays the park is still buzzing at four in the afternoon. Everywhere are people jogging, sitting on the grass, kids playing on the skateboard rink. Too many people and my enthusiasm disappear into thin air. Fat kid on a bike, fat kid on the bike. The litany starts up again.

"Here, put it around your neck. I get a practice run first." Amelia is holding up a stopwatch motioning for me to put it on.

"Where did you get the stopwatch?" Suddenly my suspicions were not so unfounded. "You planned this."

Amelia is too well mannered to mind the accusation since it is the truth. "Adam gave me the stopwatch when he left because you owe him. He would not tell me what, I decided to keep it and find out what you owe him. I figured it out – it is the Anaconda, is it not? What did you promise?"

"Not your business. Go pester the Anaconda."

"Keep it safe." She drops the watch in my hands and takes off for the starting point. "Tell me when I can go."

"Don't you want to practice first?"

"This is a practice run. I want to lay down a base time. Are you ready?" Her eyes are fixed on the Anaconda, determination written all over her face.

I press the button: "Go." Silently I pray that Amelia's practice run is not faster than my best time.

Ballet training and being a natural athlete give Amelia an unfair advantage. She whips through the fangs at breakneck speed. A high pitch squeal accompanies her first belly button jump. She momentarily hesitates at the height of the bulging stomach but makes the jump down, over-shoots the first few ribs, but she steadies herself and continues onward. She stops short of the tail.

"No, you have to go up the ramp and stop at the top of the tail! Quickly! Go!"

Amelia backs up and storms up the ramp and stops just in time before she drops off on the other side. "What is my time?"

"You did well. Take a guess."

Breathing fast, she surveys the length of the Anaconda. "Four minutes."

"Close – Four minutes and seven seconds." Definitely better than my first run but I'm not telling her that.

"I'll be down to four minutes on my next run, and then I'll chase you down, little brother. Show me what you can do." Amelia reaches for the stopwatch. "Go, I want to ride again. Why do you not start at the tail end? Would it not be easier to start at the top then you can pick up speed going through the fangs in the end. Gives you a faster time."

I wanted to know the same thing. As usual, Adam had a perfectly logical answer to the question. "Adam says there is no hole in the tail. How are you going to get inside the snake? Besides, you are supposed to turn around on the ledge and come back here again."

"That is just crazy." She eyes the tail end. "It is not wide enough to turn around. It is not possible."

I reluctantly tell her the solution. "Not turn, jump in the air turning the bike around."

She stares at me in quiet disbelieve. Then I tell her the second option. "When you get to the top of the ramp, go onto your front wheel, and swing the back onto the flat part, then you can get back down again." A calculating look enters her eyes. "No. Do not even think about it. You need a special bike with a reinforced front wheel."

"So it is possible. Just not with these bikes."

She keeps looking at the tail end. My stomach clenches and I know something terrible is coming. I do not know this daredevil side of Amelia. It scares me, she is supposed to be the responsible one.

"Three minutes and fifty-eight seconds. Do you think you can make better time today?"

The change in her thought processes makes me dizzy. I'm just happy that she is no longer interested in the tail end. To keep it in the present, I boast: "I can do three minutes and fifty-five seconds easy."

"Show me. Three seconds is much longer than you think." She holds the watch ready.

I take a deep breath. Adam's instructions are running through my mind, I firmly fix my gaze a few meters ahead of the bike. Another deep breath and on the signal, I'm off to either get my ass kicked or do the fastest Anaconda run ever.

I slip as smooth as butter through the fangs, time the belly buttons correctly, make good time on the scales even the height of the belly does not have me hesitating, and although I scrape past the last two ribs, I keep going until a bone-jarring stop sets me on top of the tail.

"You did it, Davey!" Amelia's arms are doing an up and down victory dance on my behalf.

"Time, what is my time?" I can barely formulate a full sentence, my breath coming in gasps.

"Three minutes and fifty-five seconds. Just as you predicted. Wow, that was a perfect run. My turn now."

"Wait! Take a picture of me and the stopwatch. I told Adam that I'll do the Anaconda in three-minutes and fifty – five seconds. And I did it!"

I waste no time in sending the picture off to Adam.

A few seconds later, a message bounces back. *You promised and you did it! Wow. I challenge you. I ride my bike with Father every day.*

Sure enough, there is a photo of a happy smiling Adam and The Advocate... Even the high and mighty advocate can crack a smile.

"You do not like his dad much?" Amelia is looking over my shoulder at the phone. "His mom told us about your first meeting; she thought it was sweet when you took on The Advocate because he made Adam cry. Like Adam was your kid brother." She looks me up and down. "You have changed a lot these past months."

I do not like her scrutiny, I put away my phone, avoiding her eyes. "You mean, I lost weight."

"No, not just the weight. You are confident, assertive. Taking on the bullies and not backing down." The next moment Amelia hugs me. "I like this new Davey. Just do not grow up too fast."

I do not know what to do or say and awkwardly pats her arm. Thankfully, the moment does not last long, and Amelia takes off for another go at the Anaconda.

She did not let up until she hit four minutes. I manage to repeat my best time one more time, but at the end of the long afternoon, I mostly managed to stay just ahead of four minutes and seven seconds. Where do Amelia and Adam get all the energy from?

The next day I could barely walk while Amelia waltzes gracefully down the stairs without any trouble. Perfectly attired in a green floral dress, ready to meet Grandma Edith and Grandpa Heinz. She waited until I step off the last stair. Each step pulling on aching muscles, even my stomach has suddenly developed a muscle that pulls every time I lift my leg.

"Mom, please tell Davey to change his shirt. He is carrying his breakfast with him."

I look down and immediately spots the yellow blob on the seam. Why did I not see it earlier? "You could have told me before. You are just mean." I give Amelia a dirty look and try to scrub the blob from my white T-shirt, hoping that it would not be so obvious.

Dad is not having any of this. "Upstairs, David. Change now."

By the time I made it up the stairs and changed my shirt, they have arrived. I try to slip in unnoticed, but Grandma Edith has eyes in the back of her head.

"My goodness, David. Look at you. So healthy-looking and you lost weight."For once, Grandma Edith sounds pleased with me. Her hands-on my arms, she pulls me in for a quick kiss on the forehead. She's not a hugger.

"Hello, Grandma." She still looks the same, a wiry, slim, straight back woman that carries her years well. Steel-grey piercing eyes. Hair in a neat silver bun. Dark blue travel suit with a white blouse and a pearl choker. She looks me over. "You got your Grandpa Heinz built. Going to be a big man. Look, Heinz, he is taking after you."

The chair creaks when Grandpa Heinz stands up. Dad is tall, but Grandpa Heinz is taller, broader in the shoulders. He towers over us all and fills the room with his presence. The sun glinting off his white hair.

"David." He rumbles my name. His arms are wide open. His blue eyes so like Dad and Amelia's crinkles at the corners when he smiles a welcome. I slip past Grandma, the next moment, my feet left the ground when Grandpa pulls me into a hug of enormous proportions. He smells of spice and butterscotch. I stretch my arms as far as I can, but still, I cannot fully reach around him. Grandpa just laughs and put me down. "Still need to grow a bit. You look good." There is no criticism when he looks me over, nodding approvingly. "Hank, your boy is going to grow up tall."

"Just watch the weight." I did not mind Grandma's Edith little dig. Standing next to Grandpa and Dad, I feel ten feet tall and proud to be a Miller.

Year 1; Month 5; Week 20
Captain David Zacharias Log
Stardate 71351.0. Log Entry 133. Week 20.

Operation code name: Cemetery Run
1) St Michaels is looming. Adam is back and not too happy with the training program, but I laid down the law. My way or no way.
2) My birthday is happening this week. The less said, the better.
3) Weight loss – Mom is reaching new heights. Even Grandma Edith is impressed. When she tasted Mom's special oats with the sweet red apple, crunchy pecan and coconut shavings, yoghurt, and honey drizzle, she went: "Marion, such a tasty innovation but surely too rich for breakfast." Mom just smiled because Grandma ate every single bit and scraped her bowl squeaky clean. I loved it when Grandpa went behind her back and used his finger to clean out the pot.

The day of my twelfth birthday arrives bright and sunny. Everything is conspiring to cheer me on. I should be happy – at least no party. Still, the family is pitching up in droves, not even Grandma Edith is acting as a deterrent. Adam wished me a happy birthday at one minute past twelve. I did not want to burst his bubble by telling him that I was only born at nine on this day.

I reluctantly drag myself out of bed. My cousin Liam is still snoring away, earphones tugged firmly around his head. He is sixteen years old and lives in his own world that revolves around his phone and the ever-present earphones. He has grunted his greeting on arrival and since then only spoke to his peeps on the other end of the phone. Lucky for me. His twin sisters are sharing with Amelia, and they never stop talking. Perfect Amelia is back and is totally ignoring me.

When I open the door, I can hear the girls going down the stairs. I creep on silent feet to the bathroom only to meet face to face with a bleary-eyed, Uncle Shaun.

"Heehaw birthday boy. Happy returns on this day. Put it here." I gingerly shake his still wet hand, he pulls me close for a pat on the back. Glad we met up after he has already brushed his teeth. "You getting ready for the ladies. Lots of kisses today." He winks at me and vacates the door allowing me to enter.

That basically sets the tone of the day. Clammy hugs from the uncles and perfumed kisses from the aunts with exclamations of either "You are wasting away, what is your mom feeding you?" usually the more portly ones and "Finally growing into your weight!" from the skinny ones.

After breakfast, I tried to escape next door, but Dad saw me. Liam and I were charged with setting up the barbeques and stacking the wood. The ever-present earphones must be playing music as Liam's head bobble up and down while he carries around the bags filled with wood with a few dance paces thrown in between. Finally, everything was to the uncles' satisfaction lounging on the stoep

When I go upstairs to change my T-shirt, the twins catch me in a double hug and present me with a bright blue wrapped package. "Open it," orders Bree, she has always been bossy.

Kay the quiet one explains: "It is for today. You can wear it to the party." She reminds me of my mom, especially when her single dimple puts in an appearance.

"Quickly now." Bree again.

I do as she ordered and open the package, wanting to get this over. I do not like to be the centre of attention.

Finally, the paper gives way to reveal a Converse All Star T-shirt in red and black. It is love at first sight, but then I remember that usually, gifts are either too big or too small.

"Put it on." Bree pushing again.

"I'm dirty and sweaty from carrying the wood and charcoal." I show her my hands.

She wrinkles her nose: "So it was you smelling like that."

Kay shoves her away. "She jokes. You are fine. And it would fit perfectly." She must have seen my disappointment. "We had insider information. Common, Bree, let the birthday boy get himself cleaned up. Grandma Edith is going to have a fit if we do not get to the kitchen this minute." She pulls on her twin's arms and the two dark heads disappear down the stairs. Wonder what Grandma cooked up for the twins to do. And for the second time today, I shower.

Ms McKenzie and Adam arrived at four, the advocate had an urgent phone call; he will join us later. Adam could not wait to give me my present.

"Here, Slim, this is for you. You will love it. Oh, and happy birthday again." He grabs the oversized flat gift; his mom is carrying and pushes it into my hands. "Please, open it."

"Adam, you must put the present with all the others. Davey will open it later," cautions his mom.

I can see that option does not appeal to him at all. Since I'm wearing the twins present already, which fit surprisingly well, I slip my finger under the paper flap and lift it. Small fingers start picking at the cello tape, his mom tries to stop him, but I shake my head. Adam's enthusiasm is too infectious, I have missed the little guy. Together we open the huge framed poster.

"Do you recognise it? Can you see it? I told Father you would know immediately." Adam is holding his breath, waiting for my answer.

The poster is, actually, a large town map. I could not see the farm name as it was obscured by a large envelope. So no clue there. I check the centre but no Church Street running through this town. I look at Adam, his gaze keeps straying to the right, and suddenly I know. I check, and right there at the edge of the town is a church site and the road starting out from it – St Michaels. When our town, halfway up the Magaliesberg, was created, the miners were a rebellious lot. Working, drinking hard, and partying even harder late into the early morning hours. When the church fathers tried to put a stop to it, they found themselves banished to the outskirts of the town. The god-fearing people followed them and setup homes along the road leading back into town. In the early days, we must have been the only town in South Africa with no church at its centre. History put the police station and jail in the middle.

"Wow, thank you, Adam, this is amazing. Where did you get this one? It even shows the river and the old railway."

"Father got it from the National Archives. Open this, it is another surprise." Adam holds out the big envelope. It is quite thick and properly cello-taped. I finally managed, after a bit of a struggle, to tear open the envelope along the side. Inside is a neatly folded plan. When I open it up, it is a topographical map – a blank canvas for a new town.

I give Adam a quick hug. "Thanks, Adam, Ms McKenzie, these are amazing presents and very special. Thank you so much. I'll go put this in my room to keep them safe."

"Can I come too? I want to see your room. Please, Mommy." When his mom nods, he picks up the envelope and waits for me to maneuverer the huge map up the stairs.

Inside my room, he scans it from side to side. Then he turns around. "Your room is huge. Do you always keep it this neat? That is a funny desk. Why is your desk standing up? Do you put it flat when you work?"

The whole corner of my room is taken up by a vast light green technical drawing board. I put the map next to the wall and take the envelope from Adam. I unfold the topographical map and clip it to the drawing board. When I move the T-square over the paper, Adam understands what the strange upright table with the blocks marked on it is used for. When the municipality moved from technical drawing boards to computer-aided drafting, they sold the boards and Dad bought one for me. Sometimes planning a town out by hand on paper allows more freedom. I do not think I will ever part with the board.

"Wow, this is amazing." Adam could barely reach the T-Square, but that does not deter him from trying to move it. I lower it a bit, he slides it over the map stopping at points that interests him. "Will you let me watch you draw a town sometime?"

I never had anyone showing an interest in my hobby, suddenly I'm embarrassed. "Sure, if you want to. It might be boring, you know."

"I don't mind. Just tell me when, and I'll ask Mommy. I promise to be very quiet."

I just laugh. Adam and quiet don't go together. "Common, let's go. Mom promised that we can have cake when you get here. It is called a hummingbird cake. It is made with banana and pineapple."

"That is a strange cake – does it look like a salad? Will you put candles on it? What colour are your candles? Mommy says there are lots of pink candles out there. Do you have pink candles?"

I let Adam rattle on. I missed all his crazy questions. When he finally spies the cake, he makes a beeline for it and reports back: "It looks just like a regular cake. The banana and the pineapple must be inside. You have blue and yellow candles. You must be glad your mom could not find pink candles." He looks over his shoulder when he makes the pink comment. Devils dancing in his eyes. "Mommy says that one day you are going to love pink."

"Adam, that enough. Mind your manners."

While we were upstairs, the advocate has shown up. Adam immediately clams up and goes to greet everyone by shaking their hands. Then he sees Grandpa Heinz in front of the braai, the irrepressible Adam pops out again.

"Are you a giant? Did you eat lots of vegetables when you were a kid? What kind of vegetables did you eat? Did you have to drink milk too?"

No one says a word. Everyone is watching Grandpa and the tiny curly-haired boy that barely reaches his belt. When Grandpa's deep rumbling laugh starts, Adam goes: "You sound like a real giant too."

"And where did you find this other giant, little man?" Grandpa hunches down, but Adam still has to look up to meet his eyes.

Adam shakes his head. "He is not real, he was in a movie. Movies are not real. What is your name?" Adam holds out his hand. "I am Adrian Sullivan McKenzie the fourth. But you may call me Adam."

Adam's hand completely disappears into the giant's hand. "I am Gunther Heinrich Ubert Miller, the eighth. You can call me Grandpa Heinz."

"Ok." Adam turns to my dad, looks back at Grandpa, at Dad again, then he looks at me and opens his mouth to impart his observation.

Whatever Adam wanted to say got cut-off by his mom's hand. "Look, Adam, the candles on the cake are lit. Davey is going to blow them out while he makes a wish. Go stand at the table" and she pushes him in the direction of the cake table.

Now everyone is looking at me. I suddenly do not know what to do with my hands. Must I put them in my pockets, on the table, behind my back? I stare at the cake, trying to avoid their eyes, and feel my face heat up. I just want to get this over with.

Adam pats my hand. "I was not going to say anything rude. I wanted to say that I'm glad you are my friend even if you grow up to be a giant too. There is a good chance, you know. Your dad is very tall."

I could not help smiling. "And don't you ever forget that, Adrian Sullivan McKenzie the fourth."

Adam just laughs at me. "What are you going to wish for?"

"If I tell you, it will not come true."

"Then tell me after it has come true. Now blow out your candles so that I can taste your salad cake." I blow out the candles hoping in my heart of hearts that birthday wishes really come true.

It is late. The evening is winding down. The adults are quiet, the soft murmur of the teenagers' conversation the only sound drifting on the night air. Adam has fallen asleep in Grandpa Heinz's lap. He did not even wake when the Advocate picked him up to go home. All the excitement must have tired him out. Although I still hate the thought of having a birthday party, I'm glad that Adam's first real party was mine. The only bad thing still haunting the party is the big bowl of sweets that keep growing with each present I open. Yummy chocolate bars; deliciously round Lindt truffles; bubbly minty Aero's, soft caramel toffees, homemade fudge, pink and white coconut ice, even the popcorn a sweet, sticky caramel. This is what I fear the most. A sweet-smelling temptation that is getting harder and harder to resist.

Mom did an excellent job with the healthy party food-stuff. Besides the fantastic hummingbird cake with cream cheese, lemon, and nut topping, she made the most deli-cious dark chocolate and pistachio bars. I helped her make tasty yoghurt ice lollies, some with oranges, strawberries, and my favourite naartjies. The sweet taste of the naartjie was offset by the sour yoghurt, yummy. Adam definitely likes the strawberry lollies; he has eaten two. For some salty snacks, Grandma came up with thinly sliced potato and sweet potato chips grilled to perfection with either Aromat or salty vinegar sprinkle. The twins put together fruit sosaties with small cheeses in between. There were even some tangy cocktail onions, sweet pepper, and Edam cheese and gherkin sosaties. For the mains, we grilled mealies and tomatoes on the vine.

Dad marinated the chicken in a chilli sauce for the braai. Grandpa outdid himself with apricot jam and Malay curry snoek with French bread toast. Everybody cleaned their plates and asked for seconds. I also did. But now the bowl of sweets is still sitting on the low table next to all the presents. I'm hypnotised by it. I even counted them in the firelight, twenty-two chocolate bars; six small bags of caramel popcorn; one large bag of cinnamon sugar pop-corn, two large bags of jellies. I think jellies are ok – they have zero fat, if I'm not mistaken. Maybe just one sweet treat...

"I'll go and make us a nice cup of coffee. Come, David – you can carry the tray for me." Grandma Edith must have seen that the temptation was getting too much and firmly takes me by the arm and marches me to the kitchen. "Time to get ready for bed, young man. There is church tomorrow."

I escape upstairs.

I am riding my bike with Jennie, wearing my new converse T-shirt. It feels too small, and my stomach pushes it up higher. It fitted yesterday, why does it not fit today? Then I realise that the massive bowl of sweets is in front of me. And I'm stuffing my face, while the bike is moving on its own. Jennie is talking to me, but I could not hear what she is saying, the sweets are crunching way too hard. I swallow and wait for her to repeat whatever she is saying. My hand continues to search for a minty chocolate bar.

"Do not listen to them. Stop eating. Please, Davey, do not do this. Stop."

I look around; the side of the road is lined with everyone I know.

Grandma Edith, with her mouth in a thin line, keeps saying: "I know he could not resist. Shame on you, Bubbles, you could not save the kid from himself."

Mom is looking defeated while Grandma berates her on and on. Where is Dad? He is supposed to protect Mom. Grandpa Heinz just stands there looking sad. The witch from down the street is laughing and keeps putting large green beeshart tomatoes in a basket. When she holds out the basket to me, they turn into cherry red toffee apples.

"Tricked you good – fat boy. Thought you could lose weight, but you are weak. One party and you are fat again."

Amelia is standing next to her with a stopwatch. "You are growing fatter by the minute. Look." she holds out the watch to me.

Instead of showing the time, the clock face is showing kilograms adding up. I'm still stuffing my face, unable to stop.

Suddenly Adam stands in the road, he is crying. "You promised. You promised that when you lose weight that we will go down St Michaels. Now that you are fat again, we are never ever going to. I'm going to die because you broke your promise. The advocate appears and scopes Adam up. "Do not cry – I'm your father. I will not break my promise like Davey. I'll bike down St Michaels with you. He is just a lazy, lying, fat kid on a bike."

The sound waves of my uncles and aunties, cousins chanting reaches me "Eat, eat." They are holding out hands full of sweets. Then I see my dad. He is sitting at his desk, his head in his hands. I try to tell him to save Mom, but he just sits there. I keep calling him desperate for him to do something, anything.

Then he looks up: "You failed again, and my wife is paying the price. You are a failure." He stands up and walks out of the room. I try to see where he is going, but Sunny is there with her tiger swords and Big Henry with the wild dogs at his side.

She points her blades at me: "Kill him. He is going to eat Jennie," When I look down I see that I have Jennie's arm in my hand and there are teeth marks..."

"Hey, Davey! Wake up, man."
Liam is standing next to my bed. He is still shaking me.
"Liam. Liam stop! I'm awake now."
"Ok. You are having a nightmare, Dude. Told you not to eat so much meat. It gives you nightmares, you know."

144

The last bit comes out muffled as Liam pulls the blanket over his head. Within minutes, his soft even breathing fills the room.

I'm too rattled to fall asleep. If I were alone, I would work on one of my town layouts, but with Liam here I can only trace the dark lines on the map that is still standing next to my bed. I watch the room slowly lights up when the sun finally chasing away the night. When I hear Mom going down the stairs, I slip out and follow her down.

"Davey. You are up early. Is everything ok?" Mom has put on the kettle and is busy placing cups in a tray. She leaves everything to lay a questioning hand on my forehead.

"I'm ok. A nightmare woke me up. I could not sleep again."

Mom is still trying to comb my hair into a semblance of a style but pauses when she hears about the nightmare.

"What is wrong, Davey?" I see myself reflected in her brown eyes. "Tell me about the dream; I'm your mom, I can help."

"It's that humongous bowl of sweets that is giving me nightmares." Mom starts to laugh. "Why are you laughing? This is very serious." I'm not impressed with her making fun of the issue at hand.

"I know, Davey, sorry. I was worried about the same thing."

I could not believe it. Did Mom really think I could not resist the temptation? "Why would you think that I'm so weak that I would not be able to keep away from the sweets? I am a Miller too. I can also stand my ground."

"Davey, Davey, calm down."

I try to push past her. Not again. I thought we were in a good place now; that we understand each other. We are in

145

the same boat, but she is laughing at me and think I'm weak! My nightmare for real this time.

"Davey, stop and listen to me." Mom is also giving no quarter and refuses to budge. I try to calm down. "I did not laugh at you but at the situation. I was also dreaming about that bowl of sweets the whole night. The sweets were climbing the stairs trying to reach me. We are safe. Grandma Edith appointed herself guardian of the bowl and took it away. It was the wi… Tannie Kotie who suggested that it might be prudent to remove such temptation from our sight."

I can just hear the witch saying those words. For once in my life, I'm thankful to the interfering old woman.

"So it is gone. The whole bowl – everything gone?" Then a moment of panic. "Won't they think we ate everything during the night while they were sleeping when they see the bowl is empty?" Mom shakes her head and points to the cupboard. On the top shelf is a bottle filled to the brim with sweets.

"It is still here. Why?" My moment of happiness deflates quickly. Seems like I'm not going to get rid of the temptation that easily.

"Do not worry, Grandpa Heinz closed the lid. No one but he will be able to open it."

I can breathe again.

After Mom did the rounds with the cups, the two of us sit down on the steps leading from the back door. Enjoying our green tea with a dash of lemon and sweeten with honey. This is nice, this quiet moment before the family descends on us again for breakfast.

"Mom, what does the key unlock?" Mom and Dad gave me a little red and blue box with a key in it for my birthday, but I never got around to ask what it is for. I thought it was perhaps the key to my room, but it did not fit in the lock.

Mom stands up. "Do you have the key with you?"

I take the key from my pyjama pocket. "Yes."

"Follow me." Mom walks in the direction of the garage. She stops next to the storeroom, where Dad keeps all his tools. Strictly off-limits to everyone but Mom.

"Mom?"

She is smiling, the dimple making her even more beautiful. "Happy birthday, my Davey."

I hesitantly tried the key, and the lock smoothly clicks open. The door swings open on silent hinges. I step inside and could not contain a high pitch squeal escaping me.

A brand new bike! The sun reflects off the shiny orange body. It makes the name glow with an unearthly light: *Avalanche* and small letters underneath *Cosmic*. Wow! This is a fantastic bike with an 18-speed gear shift. No more working my ass off to get up a hill. I was always envious of Adam and his 7-speed Raleigh that makes him fly uphill. He is going to be in for a fat surprise when I show up on my new bike. I touch the low black handlebars with reverence. I pull on the gear shift, moving it up and down. The bike is beautiful, from the reflectors on the back guard to the light in front. I wish there was time for me to take it out for a ride. I take one last look and turn to give Mom a hug. Dad has joined us while I was inspecting the bike.

"Thanks, Mom, Dad, this is a fantastic present. Thank you. Thank you." I give them both a quick hug and turn to look at my bike again. "Wow, this is an unexpected surprise. I love it. Wait until I show Adam. He is going to be so jealous. Eighteen speed." Then a thought crossed my mind – this bike must have cost a ton of money. "Dad, I promise to take good care of it."

Dad puts his hand on my shoulder and walks closer to inspect the bike. "Happy birthday, David. You deserve a new bike with all the hard work you put into losing weight. I know that you will take good care of it. I'm glad you like the bike; I got a good price for it. It is second-hand. James's son did not like the colour."

I look at my bike, bright burnished orange in the early morning sun. How could he not like the colour? It is the colour of adventure, fierce and burning. Now I sound like Adam. "Dad, I'm glad he did not like the colour because I love it. Could I please go for a ride – I'll be very quick, just once around the block. I promise. Please, Dad."

"Ok. Fifteen minutes, Davey, and I'm timing you."

I do not waste a second. I push the light as air bike out of the workroom to the front of the garage. Everything is perfect. Dad must have set up the bike seat at the same height as my old bike – he is like that.

The feeling is amazing. The handlebars are a bit lower, but by the time I reach the end of the driveway, I'm a pro. Dad opens the gate; I take off at a slow pace while every fibre in my being wants to race around the block at full speed. As soon as I turn the corner, sure that Mom and Dad can no longer see me, I push down on the pedals and race down the sidewalk. It is still early on a Sunday morning, and in the quiet, I can hear the tires singing on the pavement. For a single moment in time, I do not care who sees me. It does not matter – I'm a fat kid on a kick-ass bike. And right then and there, I decide I'm ready for St Michaels.

I do not remember a single word of the sermon. I keep playing the feeling of the early morning bike ride in the crisp air over and over again with a silly grin on my face.

Amelia keeps looking at me and frowning at my out of place behaviour. I could not care less. I'm happy.

Sunday lunch is a big affair since most of the uncles, aunts, and cousins will leave later today. Uncle Shawn and Aunty May have departed right after breakfast before church. They are not of the church-going Irish, according to Grandma Edith. The two sisters, Aunties Mary and Salie, left after tea and before lunch. They do not like driving in the dark. Uncle Werner, Dad's nephew, and his scandalous new wife and their two spoiled brats will leave after lunch. She does not look much like an aunt, more like a model in her high heels and denim shorts. She is beautiful, with big blue eyes and golden blond hair, but not very friendly. They stayed at a nearby B&B since, according to Aunty May: Mom's house is not good enough. But it seems the food is – they are here for lunch. The Turtle-family, as Uncle Fitz likes to call them because they always come in their Winnebago, will only leave tomorrow. Liam and the twins will also stay until Monday.

The table is loaded and not with the good stuff. The Aunties are pulling out all the stops for Sunday lunch. There are four different kinds of meat: beef meatballs, frikadelle, as we call them, in a thick brown gravy with lovely mushroom bits, fried chicken with honey and mustard drizzle, pork chops with steamed apple, and ostrich fillets in plum sauce. The vegetable selection: potato salad with crispy bacon bits, golden brown baked potatoes with a salty crust, mash potato, tomato salad with red onions and parsley, copper-penny salad, buttery and glossy, carrots and peas, beetroot in white cheese source and fresh organum, beetroot, brie and pear salad with walnuts. I do not even want to know what is for dessert.

When the eating bell sound, I make sure that I stand next to Mom to get advice on what to choose from this overflowing, delectable table.

"Mom…, what am I going to eat? There is too much food here."

She must have heard the panic in my voice: "It is ok, Davey. I'll dish up for you. Please go and get the water pitchers from the kitchen and put one on each table."

I place the last water pitcher with the cucumber and lemon slices on the kids' table and turn around to find Mom with a plate loaded up with all my favourites. And I mean loaded, there is so much food. "Mom? This is too much food."

Mom's eyes are dancing, but she is keeping a straight face when she whispers in my ear, "Small plate, Davey, do not worry. There is suddenly no more big plates left."

I sit down and take a deep breath. With my eyes close in prayer, I savour the rich aromas of the food wafting tantalisingly from my plate. I can smell the sweet pears, the vinegar in the copper-penny salad, the earthy tones of the beetroot, salty potatoes, and, above all, the aroma of fried meat. Roasted ostrich medallions covered in a dark plum source with a hint of chocolate. The first bite puts me in heaven, and I stay there all through the meal.

I'm listening with half an ear to the girls chatting, watching Liam wolfing down his food, oblivious to the world around him. I can see the little pod in his ear. Grandma Edith is going to have a fit when she sees him. He suddenly looks up, his green eyes catching mine. He waves his fork in the direction of my plate and lifts his eyebrow in question.

I mouth back: "Slow down, enjoy the food." He just grins and takes a large bite of his frikkadel. He is in great shape, especially for a guy who does not seem to do much while eating his parents out of their savings. By the time I finished my plate, the aunties are ready with dessert. It seems sanity has prevailed; ice cream is the only dessert on the menu. But make no mistake, it is no ordinary vanilla ice cream. The aunties softened the ice cream and add delicious goodies to it before freezing it up again in mini-bread tins. There is vanilla with nuts; chocolate drops and cranberries; vanilla with orange, naartjie, and lime zest; vanilla with ginger crumble. I cannot resist and beg for a taste of each - three scoops of creamy naughtiness that disappeared way too fast.

Our family has a Sunday rule, once all the tables are cleared and the dishes washed, the kitchen put to rights – the guests depart. Those that stay behind will spend the afternoon in quiet contemplation. The emphasis on quiet. Perfect Amelia and the twins spread a blanket and cushions in the shade of the large Jacaranda for an afternoon nap if they can stop talking that long. I retreat to my room. Liam has already passed out face down on the twin bed. I check my watch; it is now ten past two – a long way to go to four. I'm restless; the anticipation of seeing Adam and showing him my new bike does not allow me to stay still. I finally find myself in front of the map on the drawing board. I lazily draw my fingers along the river, the tiny streams; follow the contour of a big hill. Adam is going to be so excited when I tell him that we are ready for St Michaels. We should do it on a Sunday afternoon – there will be less traffic at that time. I wonder what he is going to say about my new bike. I check my watch again—five past three. I cannot wait any longer and decide to whatsapp Adam. He immediately responds.

I'm bored. Are you drawing your new town? Can I come and watch? Can I call you?

No – let's go biking. Do u think ur mom will let you go?
Yes. Slept late this morning and cannot sleep now. Meet
u at the gate. I have to put on my ninja suit.

I make it safely out of the house, taking care to stay behind the hedge in case the advocate spots me. He might not like this change in routine. Adam finally puts in an appearance. No Ms McKenzie.

"Adam, you did ask your mom if you can come?"

"Yes, I promise. Really. Mommy gave me the key to the small gate. Can you open it for me; it is difficult with the bike." I hesitantly take the key; a movement at the window reveals Ms McKenzie watching us. When she sees me looking, she gives a quick wave.

"Oh, double wow. Where did you get a new bike? Is it your birthday present? Can I touch it?" Adam does not wait for an answer. He reverently touches the gleaming amber bike sparking in the afternoon sun. "How many gears? Is it very fast? Can I maybe ride on it one day? This is a big bike, I need to grow up first. It is like a giant bike. Did you name your bike? What did you name your bike? I cannot wait to see how fast you can now ride the Anaconda." All the while, his small hands lightly touch here and there, clearly in awe of my superbike.

"It is an Avalanche Cosmic with eighteen gears. I do not know how fast it is yet. I only have it this morning since before church, so not much time for a bike ride. Wanna give it a workout? I thought the Amelia would be a good track to try out the gears, with all its twists and turns. You will have to help since it is the first time I have a bike with gears."

"Really, your first-time ever-ever? I'll show you. Look, the lower numbers are the low gears, and higher numbers are the high gears. First gear is low gear, eighteenth gear is high gear. When you go uphill, you use the low numbers. When you go downhill, you use the high numbers. My bike is good for uphill in two or three, and downhill, I use four. I bet the Firefly will be amazing in any gear. You just have to play around. Start in the middle." Adam easily switches the gears for me.

"Firefly?"

"Yes; your bike is all twinkling and shiny in the sun, like a firefly at night. Do you like the name?" Adam tilts his head to one side and watches me anxiously.

"I kind of like it. It is also the name of one of my favourite Sci-Fi TV series. Firefly it is. You ready to go?" Happiness spreads across his face and with a quick dip of his head; he is off in the direction of Amelia's.

Firefly is superb, like a horse raring to go. For the first time, the uphill is not such a battle with Adam racing ahead with me struggling to catch up. Now I stick to his tail. When I use the right gear, I make good time. It takes some time to learn how and when to switch the gears, but after the fifth intersection on Amelia, I get the hang of it. For the first time, I do not feel out of control going downhill. I can control my speed and beat Adam twice, racing down. My legs finally give out, and we take a breather under the trees on Kappertjie Street. Adam puts up his legs against the tree and searches the blue sky for a stray cloud to name. Adam loves naming things. If I were into reincarnation, I would think that Adam was the Adam from the Bible hence his naming issues.

"Adam, why do you want to go down St. Michaels?"

Adam takes his time, thinking it over before putting the words together. "I made a promise. To God..."

I sit up, a cold shiver travels up my spine. "Adam, you cannot make a bargain with God. It is a sin – a grave sin."

Adam turns his head, his brown eyes all earnest innocence. "No, not a bargain. Like a thank you to God because I'm better now and I have a friend."

I'm not convinced. I can hear Grandma Edith in my head – you do not bargain with God, end of story.

"You still promised to do something if God does something first – that is a bargain."

"No, it is not." Adam is also sitting up now. "I'm saying thank you to Him for keeping me safe and healthy, for bringing back my father, giving me a friend, for making life good. It's like, like those people going to their holy place. They visit this black block building. It is a very special place. I can't go there. I'm a kid. St Michaels is my holy place. I'm a pilgrim."

Ok, that is a different way of looking at it. I'm quiet, thinking. Perhaps it has nothing to do with a bargain but more a spiritual journey. "Like the Muslim pilgrims that visit Mecca. I suppose Christians go to Jerusalem."

I hold up my hand when Adam wanted to talk again. "So you say you are a pilgrim? Pilgrims walk with reverence and at a slow pace, not a mad dash down a mountain of a hill."

Adam starts to laugh. Gone is the serious face – he is all joy, passion, and energy – alive. "Do you really think I can do slow? Like an old person?" He is teasing me now. "I'm me – Adam. And if I go slowly, God will know that I'm doing it to please other people and not Him. I do everything fast."

"And why am I doing this – risking my life and neck to go down St Michaels?"

"You made a promise to me. St Michael's is your church too. Your mom is singing in the choir. Mommy says she has a voice like an angel. Your dad is a deacon; I have seen him in church. You can be a pilgrim too. You can say thank you too."

I only wanted to tease him, but as usual, he turns the tables nicely on me. "I'll think about it."

Year 1; Month 6; Week 21

Captain David Zacharias Log
Stardate 71370.2. Log Entry 134. Week 21.

Operation code name: Cemetery Run
1) St Michaels is a go. We are still keeping to the training programme.
2) Birthday over and done with.
3) Bike ride with Jennie. I'm keeping my fingers crossed that everything goes well.
4) Weight loss – I'm down two pant sizes and strangely enough three shirt sizes. I thought my legs and bum are getting the most exercise – the mystery of the human body.

The school holidays are coming to an end. Grandma Edith and Granddad are staying until Friday before flying back to Germany. Grandma Edith is closely monitoring what I eat. She tells Mom and me to keep a food diary. We are doing fine, no need to go on and on about it. What is it to her if I lose weight or not? Even Mom is getting irritated with her constant interference. Her every conversation starts with food or about food.

Grandpa Hank is ok he even went with Adam and me to the park. I totally nailed the Anaconda in three minutes and fifty-four seconds flat. I do not know who was the most excited me, Adam or Grandpa. I wanted to tell Amelia, but she was entertaining Grandma Edith.

Year 1; Month 6; Week 22

Captain David Zacharias Log
Stardate 71289.4. Log Entry 135. Week 22.

Operation code name: Cemetery Run
I hate school. I really wish I was done with it.
1) St Michaels – we are on track. Firefly makes it so much easier getting uphill. Love my bike.
2) Bike ride with Jennie. No escape now.
3) Adam's birthday – working on his gift...
4) Weight loss – still on track. Mom is going to a lot of trouble to put healthy stuff in my lunch box. I really like the health bars she makes with nuts, apricot, & dark chocolate. Mom sometimes puts in this white cheese – Edam, I think that really does not taste like anything at all.

I forgot how horrid school can be. I barely made it through the first period when Big Henry, Peter, and Crunch corner me on the stairs.

"What happened to you, Little Nuke? Did you explode over the holidays? Could Mommy not put you back again? Seems she missed some stuffing. You are looking a bit on the thin side." As usual, Big Henry is leading the charge.

I decide to be nice. "Hi, Henry. Did you have a good rugby tour? Win all your games?"

For a moment, he seems confused, but since our school won the competition, he could not help gloating. "You shoulda been there. We showed the others how to play rugby. Didn't we guys? Crouch had to put two guys down hard. Taught them a good lesson on the first day." He punches Crouch's upper arm pleased with his pal's rugby prowess.

"How many tries did Peter score?" Peter is our school's top try scorer. Not only does he sounds like a donkey, he also has the same stubborn streak that makes him really good on the rugby field. When he gets the ball, he wants to score a try; nothing and no one is going to stop him. Crouch and Henry act as the battering rams opening up space for him to run. While Big Henry and Peter excitedly tell me about his seven tries, I edge slowly up the stairs away from them. Just when I thought that I have made it, the Crouch finally joins the conversation.

"Why you losing weight? You sick, Man?" He leans down to inspect my face when he drops the bomb: "Love-sick for little Jennie. You missed your Chinese girlfriend all day every day."

Could it get any worse? Naturally, the other two pick up on the question and sing-song loud enough for the whole school to hear "Little Nuke has a girlfriend."

Of course, that is when Jennie's two friends show up.

Anneke, the one with her white-blond hair in a neat braid, looks me up and down, not impressed with what she sees. "Do not be silly. Fat Boy is not Jennie's boyfriend. She has standards. She only feels sorry for him." Disgust is clearly written all over her face. Her bubble-gum chewing friend agreeing on the state of affairs. I can feel the red-tide of shame rising up from my neck. In my desperate dash to freedom, I ran straight into Ms Gillian, the librarian.

"Really, Davey, you can be so clumsy sometimes. Slow down before you hurt someone."

The rest of the day, I try to avoid the curious and sometimes pitying glances. As if that is not enough, Ms Daniel comments on my weight loss in front of the whole class. I want to disappear into the floor when everyone turns around to have a good look at me and my new body. When I finally see Jennie after the second break, she walks right by me, pretending to be talking to her friends. She does not stop on her way home, but she did ring her bike bell as usual. I really wanted to tell her about my new bike. Maybe tomorrow.

I did not talk to Jennie the whole week.

Year 1; Month 6; Week 23

Captain David Zacharias Log
Stardate 71408.5. Log Entry 136. Week 23.

Operation code name: Cemetery Run
I hate school. I really-really hate school. I Hate HATE
School. Wish I could be homeschooled like Adam.

I hate, hate school. I'm even sorry that I lost weight – now I'm getting attention because I lost weight. Even the teachers are commenting. They are mostly positive, but some kids are downright negative and rude about it. By Wednesday, I had enough. When snotty Allister tells me that I'm flabby, I hit him in the mouth with my fist. So now, I'm listening to Principal van Rooyen talking about fortitude and hormonal changes and self-control. Next to me, Allister is milking the situation, holding a bloody tissue to his split lip, groaning from time to time to underline the principal's words.

"I'm sorry I lost my temper." It's a lie; the only thing I'm sorry for is not hitting him harder. We shake hands and Principal van Rooyen walks us both out.

"Davey, you do realise that next time I have to call your parents? This is not your first altercation. Mr Potgieter tells me he saw you fighting outside the school before the holidays started. I'm watching you, young man, step carefully." It was an exercise in self-control not to wipe the smirk from Allister's face when Van Rooyen left us on our own.

Still no sign of Jennie. The day of our bike ride came and went without a word from her. She will ring the bell when she passes me on the street but does not talk to me.

Perhaps she is ashamed to be associated with me. She must have decided to listen to scary Sunny. I sometimes see Sunny when we bike. She would suddenly be there under a tree, waiting at a crossing, sometimes in her white karate clothes with a black box, always watching.

Adam's chatter is getting on my nerves. The afternoon bike rides usually relaxes me, but not today. "Hey Davey, what did you decide?

"About what?"

"Why you are going down St Michael's? It has been a whole week, it is a long time – and you must know by now what you are grateful for."

"I don't know. Have not really given it any thought." I did think about it, but all the stuff going on at school made it somewhat hard to be grateful – also, the lump in my pocket.

Adam is not happy: "Why not. This is important – you are a pilgrim too? Did you not think about anything?"

I'm really not in the mood for this conversation, too much other stuff on my mind. "I go to school, Adam. I have tests and homework, stuff to do. I do not sit around all day."

Now Adam is also riled up. "I go to school to – every day from nine to two. I also write tests, Sometimes Ms Emily would say, we are writing a quiz test right now, this very minute, and I have to think really fast and remember stuff. You are older, your brain is better trained – you must have thought of something." Adam is not letting this go. "Just think of something, right this very minute. Common, Davey, just one thing to be grateful for."

"Adam, just shut up. I do not want to talk. Be quiet." Adam's bike wobbles from the onslaught.

"You are really mean today, Davey."

Even I'm shocked at what I said. This is not me. Why am I being horrible to the only person on the planet who is still talking to me? What is wrong with me? Even at school, I'm reacting to what kids are saying. Before, I would have never ever pushed or hit Allister. There must be something wrong with me. What am I turning into? I can hear him sobbing, wiping his nose on his sleeve. I know that I must apologise, but my tongue stays silent, no words to say I'm sorry.

At the end of our silent bike ride, Adam gives a small wave: "Bye, Davey."

For once, Adam does not ask if he sees me tomorrow. I say nothing at all.

In my room, I stare at the Bar One on my desk. Bought it after a stressful day at school. I have started to carry it around in my pocket. Touching it throughout the day. Just knowing it's there calms me down, but it also makes me feel guilty. I have not decided if I'm going to eat it or not.

"Did you fight with Adam?" Now Perfect Amelia is getting on my case.

"No." I barely hid the chocolate bar in time.

"Do not lie, little brother, you must have fought with Adam. Usually, the whole neighbourhood can hear the two of you coming, but not today. You know his mom is going to call our mom and then you are going to get an earful."

I eye her resentfully. "It is my business. Stay out of it."

"Davey, what is wrong with you? You are acting strangely, out of character." She comes into my room. Perfect Amelia is a light silhouette against the dark walls of my room.

"Mom, Mom! Amelia is pestering me when I want to do my homework. Tell her to leave. Please."

Mom appears behind Amelia. Today she is wearing a bright yellow dress with a navy belt, such a contrast to my dark mood. She is not smiling.

"What is it with your two?" She pins me with a stare. "What is wrong?"

I do not want to look her in the eyes. Instead, I stare at my bare feet on the white rug in front of my bed. Why do I have a white carpet in my room? Oh yeah, to learn the principles of cleanliness and neatness.

"Nothing, I'm fine." The bed dips when Mom sits down next to me.

"He is lying. He has been acting strangely since schools started up again. He is getting in trouble for fighting at school." Perfect Amelia ratting me out. I hate her.

"Ai, Davey, is it those horrible boys again? I thought this was sorted out before the school closed last quarter." Mom rubs circles on my stiff, unbending back. "My Davey, things will get better. You just have to believe. Look how far you have come."

I stand up abruptly. "Mom, I'm fine. I have homework to do. Please leave." Mom stays seated on my bed. Then she leans across and picks up my mobile phone. "Apologise." I stare at her blankly. Must I apologise to her or she'll call Dad. "Call Adam and apologise right now. I do not raise kids with no manners."

"How do you know it is me that has to apologise?" Stalling for time.

"Of course it is you. You are the only grumpy one going around fighting with everyone." I glare at Amelia.

"Go, Amelia, I have this. Here, Davey, start dialling. I'm waiting. Call him, or I take you over there to apologise in person. You are going to apologise – one way or the other." She pushes the phone at me.

"Ok. I'll do it but not with all of you hanging over my shoulder." I take the phone from her.

Mom looks doubtful, still sitting on the bed. "You promise? You know I will call Ms McKenzie to check if you did."

"Yes, Mom, I promise to apologise." But I'm definitely not calling Adam. I'll send him a text.

"While you apologise I'll go make you a nice glass of ice-coffee."

"Thanks, Mom." Anything to get her out of the room. Instead of calling Adam, I take out the chocolate Bar One, after a moment of hesitation, I tear off the paper and stuff my face. Bite, chew, swallow. I do not take time to taste the dark bitter chocolate, the sweet caramel. The bar settles heavily in my stomach. It makes me feel ill. I pick up the phone and send a quick text to Adam.

Sorry about today. We will talk tomorrow. Davey.

He answers almost immediately. *C u 2morrow, Adam.*

Typically Adam, a second later: *Hope u feel better soon. U're going to be a horrible giant when u're not feeling good.* He ends with a smiley face.

I send him an angry face.

When the gate bell rings the next day, I'm tempted not to go down and meet Adam. I change my mind once I realise that such an act would result in everyone asking questions. I have apologised after all.

Adam takes one look at my face and, without saying a word, takes off in the direction of Milk Thistle aka Hurricane Uphill number four. Adam's not talking at all. Talk about self-control. First, it is unnerving, the silence around us, I want to talk to fill the quiet space, but I have nothing to say. I listen to the sound of our tyres on the cement paving, the slight squeak of the cable when we apply the brakes, the whirly noise made by the spokes, the loudness of my breathing. I start to relax and enjoy the ride.

At the gate, we say goodbye: "See you tomorrow, Adam."

He acknowledges with a wave of his small gloved hand.

This becomes our routine – barely talking to one another. Not angry anymore but not talking. It cannot go on like this forever – something is going to give, just a matter of time.

Year 1; Month 6; Week 24

Captain David Zacharias Log
Stardate 71427.7. Log Entry 137. Week 24.

1 x Bar One
2 x Dorito's Spicy wings
1 x Gingerbread Man
1 x bag of jelly snakes
I am a big fat white whale; A fat big white whale. A white big fat whale. I am fat. I am big and fat. I am a big fat loser. I am fat.

Adam and I are still not talking. It is unnerving this quiet Adam. Despite everything, I enjoy our bike rides and barely wait for the school day to end. The highlight of my day – pathetic – a bike ride with a ten-year-old that does not talk to me.

Year 1; Month 7; Week 25

Captain David Zacharias Log
Stardate 71446.9. Log Entry 138. Week 25.

3 x 150g Smarties
2 x 85g Peppermint Aero
2 x 46g Lunch bars
2 x 45g Doritos Spicy wings
2 x 152g Oreo cookie boxes
3 x 150g sour worms

Year 1; Month7; Week 26

Captain David Zacharias Log
Stardate 71466.3. Log Entry 139. Week 26.

Fat; Fatter; Fattest…

12 x mini doughnuts
2 x 85g milk chocolate Aero
1 x 85g peppermint Aero
3 x 152g Oreo cookie boxes
2 x 46g Lunch bars
2 x 45g Doritos Spicy wings
6 x 25g Sweetie Pies

The one week flows into the next. I'm secretly eating in my room. I usually feel guilty afterwards. I eat to eat, no joy, no savouring, no tasting. Just a mechanical bite, chew, swallow until the sweets and chips are gone – day after day. Now I know why people binge eats and purge. Trying to get rid of the guilty feeling that makes the food lie heavy in your stomach, nauseous and bloated. But I don't. Amelia is next door to the bathroom and barfing is disgusting.

Mom can see I'm gaining weight. She is not saying anything, just continuing to cook healthy meals, filling up my lunchbox with healthy snacks, fresh fruit, and nutritional bars. Dad pretends not to notice, but I sometimes catch him looking at me.

Amelia is her horrid perfect self. She has found two-litre plastic coke bottles somewhere, filled them with water, and put them on my desk. I throw out the water and put the bottles in the trash. The next day there were again two bottles, and I trash them too. Neither of us is giving up.

Year 1; Month 7; Week 27

Captain David Zacharias Log
Stardate 71485.5. Log Entry 140. Week 27.

Fat; Fatter; Fattest…

2 x 85g Dark chocolate Aero's
5 x 150g Smarties
2 x 46g Lunch bar
5 x 45g cheese and onion chips
3 x 152g Ice Zoo Boxes
3 x 150g Smarties

I'm getting fatter and fatter. Maybe I will explode someday, just like Peter Wentworth predicted.

Year 1; Month 7; Week 28

Captain David Zacharias Log
Stardate 71504.6. Log Entry 141. Week 28.

6 x 150g Smarties
1 x 85g Dark chocolate Aero's
4 x 45g tomato and onion chips
1 x 46g Lunch bar
5 x 45g cheese and onion chips
1 x 152g Ice Zoo Boxes
4 x chocolate doughnuts (in one day)
I'm keeping all the food wrappers in my cupboard. Per-
haps one day I will drown in it. A big fat white whale of a
kid covered in food wrappers. Serves him right.

Maybe my descent into limbo, doing nothing, has
pushed my guardian angel over the edge and he or she decided to take matters into their own hands. I seriously think
my guardian angel is a she. Only a woman could come up
with such a devious plan. I should have been wary – the
day started off with Perfect Amelia walking me to school.
We silently walk the four blocks to school. When we
reach, Perfect Amelia continues onto the high school without saying a single word. Not even goodbye.

"I've made a decision."
I look up, shocked out of my private pity party by the
sudden appearance of Jennie at my hiding place in the library. The next moment she pushes past me and sits down
on the floor next to me. She takes the chocolate bar that I
have secretly been snacking on and continues to eat it. I
can only stare at her. I have never been this close to her. I
can see her hair has dark blond streaks in it, flecks of green

are scattered in her brown eyes, the light from the window dances on her faces. She smells like flowers and lemons.

"Do you have something to drink? That was disgustingly sweet, now I'm thirsty." I hand her my fizzy water with the cucumber and strawberry pieces in it. "I like this. Did your mom make it?" She gets comfortable, holding the bottle between her hands: "Like I said, I have made a decision."

I stare wordlessly at this strange Jennie, too afraid to blink, to move.

"I like you, David Miller. You are a nice person. Sunny agrees – you are a nice person." At that statement, I can only do the Miller eyebrow arch. Really, Sunny has decided I'm nice. When I open my mouth to ask a question, she holds up her small hand with the light pink nails. She has a tiny scar on her ring finger. I want to ask her about it.

"I am going to be your friend; not a girlfriend. Grandpa says I'm still too young to be someone's girlfriend; I have to be myself first. Friends, ok?" She hands me back the bottle. I drink without thinking. She takes the bottle, unscrews the top, and fishes out a piece of strawberry. "So, now that it is sorted, when are we going biking? Sunny says you have a smashing new bike. I can't wait to see it." Jennie is looking right at me.

"It is an Avalanche Cosmic. I call it Firefly because it sparkles in the sun like a firefly at night." I snap my mouth closed. She does not need to know that.

"I like it. When can I see it? Is Saturday ok? I can come after twelve. My mom will then be home to watch our granddad."

"No, it is lunchtime," I speak without thinking.

Jennie giggles: "You are right. Let's meet after two. Two-thirty if you are doing the dishes." Does she know about my dishwashing punishment?

"Yes. Ok. Where will we meet? I do not know where you live."

"We can meet at Kappertjie Street Island. You know where that is." I can see in her eyes she is teasing me. She must have seen Adam and me countless times taking a breather after the uphill. That reminds me, I have to let Adam know that I'm going biking with Jennie on Saturday. He might get worried if he sees me taking off on my bike without him, especially now that we are not talking.

"Ok. I'll meet you there. We can go to the park if you want to."

Jennie shakes her head: "No." She is taking small bites out of the strawberry she fished out of the bottle. "I want to show you my part of town." Her teeth are very white.

"Ok."

She pulls out another strawberry with her fingers and gives the bottle back to me. With a small wave, she walks away.

I am flying on cloud nine – Jennie has talked to me! We are going biking. Then I remember and fall in a pit of despair and loathing – I fat, not as fat as I was previously, but still fat. What am I going to do? Up to cloud nine again – Jennie wants to be my friend.

I come back to earth – hard. I have failed a test. A math test of all the things. How is it possible? Yet it is it there in my own handwriting, all the stupid mistakes. In the right-hand corner, Mr Du Plessis has left a note in his small, neat writing: 'Meeting scheduled with parents'.

Dad and Mom join me in Principal van Rooyen's office the next day. You would have thought I'll be on my best behaviour, but I got into a pushing and shoving match with Big Henry of all people on my way to the office. That is why it is a bit of a dishevelled me showing up in the principal's office for the big meeting. Another nail in my coffin courtesy of my guardian angel. I silently suffer through the intervention session focusing on seeking professional help, anti-social behaviour, and aggressive attitude. Mom sits closest to me – thin-lipped, her back ramrod straight, she is visibly upset. Next to her, Dad is saying little, agreeing here and there with the principal. He keeps patting Mom's hand reassuringly. I'm going to pay for upsetting his wife, my mother, by the grace of God.

I'm suspended for the rest of the week. That is a relief. I do not understand; usually, when someone like Big Henry and the wild dogs start shoving me around, I just stand there, taking the hits until they get tired and go away. Now, I fight back. Why do I now suddenly push back, hard? I was never like that and worse of all, I think Big Henry and the wild dogs like it. The Crunch will bump into me on purpose to see if I react. I'm not a fighter. I do not like this out of control feeling; it scares me. I'm miserable all the way home. The car is quiet; no-one is saying a word. It seems I suck all the talk out of people.

At home, Mom tells me there are extra buttons in the workroom. "Get one and fix your shirt before putting it in the wash," She turns and walks away. Dad goes back to work.

I spend the day in my room doing homework. Mom brings me water with cucumber and blueberries. She leaves without talking to me. I wonder if Jennie would eat the blueberries from the glass.

Dad left earlier without telling me my punishment. Mom is not saying a word. Perfect Amelia is ignoring me.

I cannot take it anymore. After dinner, I approach him. "Dad."

He looks up from the paper. I clear my throat and try again. "Dad, you have not yet told me what my punishment is. What do you want me to do? Am I grounded?"

Dad watches me over the paper, the light reflecting from his glasses, making it impossible for me to read his eyes. He gives a deep sigh: "No. For some reason I think you would welcome being grounded, so no, you are not grounded."

"I do not understand, Dad."

"David, if you do not actively pursue a solution to a problem, it never gets solved. Or the problem gets solved on your behalf, and the solution may not be what you want. You will have to make a decision. Take a stand and decide what you want to do. You are my son, I'm here if you need me, but I'm not going to push you into a decision or make a decision on your behalf. You had shown considerable character and perseverance when you wanted to change you're eating habits. I trust you. I'm leaving it in your hands to find a solution to the problem that you can live with every day. See this as an opportunity to make things right." He shakes out the paper and continues to read.

This is worse than getting a hiding. This belief in me that I will make the right decision. What am I going to do? That evening I sit and stare at my sweets stash for a long time. I did not eat any – Dad's words keep ringing in my head. "I trust you."

Friday dawns a bright blue sunny Highveld day. I stay in my room, doing homework, packing and unpacking drawers. I cannot find an answer to the problem of being big fat David Miller.

At four, when Adam rings the bell, the heat has not dissipated. I know we are in for a Highveld storm of epic proportions. The clouds hang black and heavy. Mom catches up with me at the door.

"It looks like a storm is coming, stick a bit closer to home today. It would not be good for Adam to get wet. The lightning is dangerous. Stay away from the trees." Mom's worried gaze follows me all the way out the gate.

"Stay close to home?" Adam must have been given the same warning as me.

"Yes. Let's go to Acacia street, there is an open space we can do some speed work." Adam takes the lead. I still marvel at the ease with which Firefly can climb the uphill. That reminds me: "Adam, I'm going for a bike biking on Saturday with a friend from school."

Adam takes a long time to answer. "Ok." I can hear from his voice that he is upset.

"I'm meeting her at two-thirty. We can still ride at four or maybe a little later. It is not getting dark so early, it might have cooled down a bit too."

"Ok. Text me when you wanna me to come." He sounds lost, without energy.

This is the most we have talked over the past weeks.

The open erf was a house once. Someone has demolished the house but left the boundary wall, the gates are gone too. The garden has taken over giving it an overgrown, sad appearance. Adam likes to pretend he is in a jungle, charging after imaginary beasts while jumping over rubble piles left there. Several paths crisscrossing the stand, made by thrill-seekers. Adam is off doing his own thing. After a while, the heat gets to me. I sit down in the shade of bougainvillaea that has escaped the wall and is climbing up a tree. Adam has found an old bath buried halfway into the ground. He is using it as a ramp to jump onto what is left of the stoep. I watch as Adam revs up, charging up the ramp and makes the jump, barely, the back wheel catches on a creeper. He wobbles dangerously, close to the edge.

"Adam, be careful!"

He rights his bike and gives me a small wave. "Come and try the jump, it is fun."

"No, let's go home, it's going to rain."

"No." Adam slowly rides his bike right up to me. He stops and just looks at me. "You are getting fat again. What about St Michaels? You promised that we can go down St, Michaels when you no longer fat. Now you are getting fat again on purpose."

I see red. "Do not call me fat! I warned you about that. Is everything always about you? Poor little Adam, sick little Adam, do you even think about anybody else's problems? Leave me alone. I was happy before I met you."

"You are a liar – a big fat liar!"

Since I cannot hit the smart mouth, I decide to go home – with or without him. I charge out of the overgrown garden, a thunderclap accompanying my uncontrolled exit. Then I hit him with my bike. For a moment, I see fireworks, bright lights dancing, a feeling of flying and then black.

When I come too, I can hear Adam crying, he is wiping my face. "Don't die, Davey. Please don't die. I swear I will never-ever-ever call you fat again. Please don't die. I'm sorry, Davey. It is ok if you are fat. Please don't die."

"Look, he is coming too, give him some air. Do not fret so much little one. He just passed out for a moment. He hit the ground pretty hard." The Italian accent sounds familiar, but it is just out of reach.

"Nooo, he is bleeding. He is going to die." Adam, arguing with the Italian.

"No head wounds bleed a lot. Just keep pressing on it."

I can feel Adam pressing down on the side of my head. He is still crying. I open my eyes and meet his teary dark browns. For a moment, we just stare at one another.

"I'm ok. Let me up."

"No. I'll take care of you – stay still." Adam presses hard on my head, trying to keep me down.

"Davey. Davey. Do not move. Let's get the bleeding under control."

I stop moving. I realise that I'm lying on the ground, my head on Adam's skinny legs. His one hand is pressing down on the side of my head. The other is alternating between wiping and patting my face. A piece of cloth is obscuring my vision, I lift a hand to move it out of the way.

"How many fingers, Davey?"

I ran-over a priest, not just any old priest. No – I had to rundown the visiting priest from the Vatican in Rome, Italy. "Fingers, Davey. How many?"

I continue to stare at the large man bending over Adam and me. A full black beard covers most of his face, he has the kindest black eyes.

"Sorry for running you over, Father."

Father Bosinio starts to laugh, a big belly laugh that bubbles up from his immense stomach and rumbles out of his mouth. "You? You ran me over. A small *bambino* like you, ran me over." He starts to laugh again, shaking his head at the absurd notion that I could possibly have run him over.

"Davey is going to be a giant when he grows up. Like Grandpa Heinz." Adam jumping to my defence.

"A giant, you say. That I must see. Fingers?"

"Three, Father."

184

"You are going to be ok. Just stay down for a bit until we stop the bleeding."

The first raindrop plops down on his cheek, for a moment it looks like the big man is crying then the drop runs into his big black beard. He looks up: "Now you send the rain."

The Father reaches behind him and opens a huge black umbrella. It covers all of us. I look at Adam, he has stopped crying, but the evidence is all over his face. The tears are washing little roads in the dirt on his cheeks. "You ok, Adam?"

"Yes, I'm ok" It does not take long for Adam to settle in. A new adventure has found him. "I have never been outside in the rain. Have you been outside when it rains?" He sticks his hand out, my eyes follow the rain spattering down on his skin. He tastes the rain and grins at me. He put his rain covered hand on my face. "It is cold, do you feel it."

I move my head, it hurts when I move it.

"Careful there, we will wait out the rain. No thunder. I was hoping for thunder. Maybe next time, mmm." The Father sighs, deeply disappointed.

Oh no. I'm stuck in the rain, under an umbrella, with two Adams.

Father Bosinio must have seen my expression. "Not to worry, *ragazzo*, your guardian angel watches over you. He sends me after all to break your fall." The umbrella tilts when he opens his arms, remembers, and settles down.

"Sorry, Father. Are you all right? I did not see you." A horrible thought pops into my head "Firefly! Is my bike, ok?"

The Father's laugh rumbles out again. "All good. The bike also good, I'm soft, big like a cushion." He checks on

185

my wound, tsk-tsk a bit and presses down. "Still leaking, hmmm."

Adam alternates between petting my cheek with his free hand and sticking it out in the rain and tasting it. He cannot stop smiling, happiness lighting up his face.

"What are you two boys doing? I see you many times, going up the hill and down the hill, up down many times."

Adam looks at me, I look at Adam. Lying to a priest is not an option, especially one as kind as Father Bosinio. We make a silent decision. "St Michaels Avenue."

After I utter the words, there is silence, while the Father considers my answer. He seems puzzled at my response; I watch as understanding dawns. Then his laughter rings out. What kind of priest is this? The umbrella is shaking from his laughter, big raindrops spatter on me. Finally, the Father pulls himself together.

Then he asks: "This is important to you. Why?"

"It like a pilgrim." It is Adam who pipes up. He tells the Father that we are athletes and that we have a training programme – using the words that I said a lifetime ago. He tells him about the five training hills – the Big Easy, the Rockies, and number three Amelia. That we are now at hill number four called Hurricane. The final one is called Ball Buster."

The Father listens attentively "Very fast pilgrimage, not much time to think. Why do you wish to make a pilgrimage?"

"To say thank you."

"Thank you for what, little man? You very young, not much life yet."

"I'm ten years old. I say thank you for being alive, not being so sick anymore, Father is back home with us, and I have a real friend." He pats me on the head.

"And you, *ragazzo*?"

186

I lay there listening to the rain drumming on the umbrella, the smell of wet soil, dust, and oil, the steam rising from the hot street. Suddenly I know what I am thankful for. "Thankful for second chances to make things right when we do not get it right the first time. Thankful for a friend that does not give up, ever, even when I am horrible to him."

Father Bosinio weighs up the answers given. In contemplation, he looks like a priest, solid, calm, peaceful. After a while, he simply says: "I'll help."

"You are too big for a bike. I do not think there is a big enough bike in the whole world."

I pump Adam in the ribs with my head.

"Davey, stay still. It is the truth, look at the Father, he is too round to fit on a bike."

"Adam!" I groaned. He finally realises his mistake.

"Sorry, Father. I was rude... but I still think you cannot ride a bike."

The Father is smiling, and I jump in before Adam can open his mouth again. "I do not understand Father, how do you mean help us?"

"Make it safe. Not safe what you are doing."

"How can you make it safe?"

"Tell the people what you are doing."

"No. You cannot do that. Mommy will say no. You cannot tell ever. Promise not to tell." Adam is close to tears, his hands clenching on the side of my head.

The Father ruffles his hair. "Calm down. I'll make it right, trust me, it is better this way."

"But Father, Adam is right. Once the grownups know, they will stop us. Dad will take away my bike." I do not even want to know what the advocate will do to me. I pull on his sleeve, desperate for him to see the seriousness of the situation. "Please, Father, do not say anything, please."

"This is like a confession. You are bound by church law; you cannot tell," Advocate Adam stating his point.

Father Bosinio shakes his big head. "Have faith, *ragazzi*, have faith."

When we want to continue to argue. The Father waves his finger. "Faith."

I can hear a sad Adam mutters: "Mommy is going to say no. Then Father is going to take my bike away. I'll never see you again. Ever and ever." I have to agree with Adam. Once the advocate hears the news, he is not going to let me anywhere near his son. I'll be probably grounded for life too. Dad will be so disappointed. I can already hear him: "Millers do not put innocents in harm's way – we are protectors. We take care of people."

Father Bosinio sits under his enormous black umbrella – a serene expression on his face. Adam and I are puddles of disappointment. Our grand adventure has come to an unexpected end. When the rain stops, the Father pulls another clean handkerchief from his voluminous robes and binds my head.

"You look like a pirate." The irrepressible Adam is at it again. I make a pirate face at him. All animosity and ill feelings between us washed away by the rain.

The Father shakes the water out of his umbrella and stows it away on his back. He gives me a hand and pulls me up. "I'll take you home. Explain to the parents." Father Bosinio taking charge.

We are a sorry bunch walking home. I was not up to ride my bike, which has thankfully not sustained any damage hitting the big soft cushion, Father Bosinio. When we turn onto our block, I can see Adam's Mom at their gate.

With the advocate. I just know that he is going to lay down the law and that means no Adam anymore. I look at Adam – he is close to tears again. When the advocate sees us, he takes long strides down the street and meets us halfway. He checks over Adam.

"Adam. Are you all right? You did not come home on time. Why did you not answer your phone?" He definitely does not look pleased with the situation.

"Yes, Father, I am fine. I am wearing my tracker watch. See…"

"This is so irresponsible of you, David. You were to come home before…" He notices my injury. His eyes narrow, now he is even angrier. "What were you doing? Did you put Adam in any danger? I do not think it is healthy for Adam to play with a kid so much older than him. This will end now."

Father Bosinio was not to be ignored any longer. "Mr. McKenzie" his voice booms out over the quiet street. "Kids are fine. We stayed out of the rain." He pulls at his robes to show that they are dry. Dusty and dirty but dry. His hands return to our shoulders, keeping us anchored to his side.

The advocate pulls at Adam's bike, but Adam has a stubborn look on his face and stays put. "Adam, we are leaving right now."

Father Bosinio, using his church voice, takes on the advocate and the advocate loses to the man of faith. It was a beautiful thing to watch. Ms McKenzie has finally caught up with us, when she sees and hears what is going on, she leans against a garden wall hiding her smile behind her hands, but her eyes give her away.

Mom and Dad, holding hands, have also joined the service. Everything about Father Bosinio is big. Gigantic, to use Adam's word. He is using his stature to his advantage to tell the tale of our afternoon adventure. By now, people have heard the commotion and are peaking through their windows. A brave few have taken up position on their stoep. His voice calls to them, his audience enthralled by the telling of our story. A story that is now a heroic quest for the Lord. He lowers his voice, and the small crowd leans in to hear, he raises his voice, and they sway back. This must be what it was like to listen to one of those Roman orators.

The way the Father tells it, he had interrupted our training session when he thoughtlessly stepped in front of my bike, which caused me to fall. He wanted me to lay down until the bleeding stopped, the rain caught us, but we are all dry and safe. He thanks our parents who have raised such selfless, mindful kids that want to give back to the community. Then he tells them about St Michael, a symbol of our faith and our quest to say thank you to the Lord. By the time he is done, the parents have agreed. The advocate grudgingly, since there were so many witnesses, all the time pinning me with a stern look. Adam could not contain his joy; he is jumping up and down, pulling my arm to join him in his crazy dance.

When Father Bosinio leaves, he whispers just one word to the two of us.

"Faith."

Year 1; Month 7; Week 29

Captain David Zacharias Log
Stardate 71523.8. Log Entry 142. Week 29.

Operation code name: St Michael's Pilgrimage
1) All everyone is talking about is St Michael's – even the kids at school know about it.
2) I could not go biking with Jennie on Saturday because I hit my head. She's busy next Saturday. So I have two weeks to lose weight.
3) I still have to finish Adam's birthday gift – I'm making him a special town map
4) Weight Loss – back on the straight and narrow

My days take on a dreamlike quality. One moment I was living my insignificant, boring life, and the next it exploded outwards. Six months ago, I was a fat kid (still fat) living on autopilot. Then I decided to try to lose weight and my whole world changed. And it is all Adam. I'm sure that I would have given up long ago was it not for the puppet hanging over our garden wall declaring that I'm his friend. At school, 'Little Nuke' is no longer derogatory. Strangers slap me on the back to say, "Go, Little Nuke!" The Pear girl tells me I'm brave beyond belief. Amelia is looking at me as if I have grown two heads. It is embarrassing. She insists on helping me to train, she tells me I have to do cardio exercises. Dad, well, he does not say a single word. Just squeezed my shoulder looking proud. Mom is doing all the talking. She keeps hugging me, calling me brave and an angel. Even the witch down the street now waves at Adam and me when we race down the road.

The only dark cloud is the advocate. He is still unhappy about the whole episode. Adam cheerfully tells me that when the advocate once again brought up my irresponsible behaviour, Ms McKenzie told him to be thankful that Father Bosinio is a priest and not an advocate – no one would stand a chance against him in court. The advocate had no answer to that. He did, however, decide to take a more active role in our training. He took over my training program and made changes 'as not to tire out Adam'. Adam had to go to the doctor to get medical clearance. Poor kid is on another special diet. Sometimes, when his schedule allows, he would join us on our bike rides. I hate it when he does that. I'm back on track, losing weight. I've given my bag of sweets to the Father, who happily took it to distribute to the needy. His words, not mine.

Year 1; Month 7; Week 30

Captain David Zacharias Log
Stardate 71542.9. Log Entry 143. Week 30.

Operation code name: St Michael's Pilgrimage
1) St Michaels – here we come.
2)Little China is fantastic. I'm glad Jennie is my friend, she's the best.
3)Adam's birthday gift is done. I hope he likes it.
4)Weight Loss – It seems easier this time around. I think I lost some of the weight I picked up when I was all screwed up.

Jennie and I finally went for a bike ride on Saturday. When I arrived at Kappertjie Street Island, she was already waiting. She looked amazing in blue jeans and a red T-shirt with white and pink flower pattern all over. Her long brown hair hanging in a curtain down her back.

"Wow. That is a kick-ass bike. The name Firefly fits it all shiny and bright. Why don't you ride it to school?"

"I like walking. Maybe next year." I still feel uncomfortable riding in public – but at least now my bike looks like it could carry my weight.

She shows me her side of town – an area called Little China. It is like a different world – the noise, smells and colours are overwhelming. It seems everyone knows everyone else on the street. They greet each other as loud as they can over the noise of the car hooters, the bicycle bells, the street food vendors, the gas stoves, and the old women yelling at children and cats alike. I make her laugh with all my questions, my round eye astonishment at the people, sounds, and food. I don't want the afternoon to end. I could not get enough of all the colours, which seems to be everywhere. Vibrant reds with gold inlay, pinks, and blues. Streets that twist and turn endlessly, small side alleys opening up in courtyards filled with houses and people. I love the smell of street food and the energy of the place. Hot steamed buns filled with meat; sticky Chinese sosaties and chewy dumplings. Jennie dares me to try the sweet tasting crab meat on a bamboo skewer. I like the crispy hot vegetable spring rolls the best – sour and sweet at the same time. I make her promise to bring me again to this magical world, where nothing makes sense to me, where I got lost after the first turn.

I am nearly late for my bike ride with Adam, but when I give him the still-warm crunchy spring roll, he has no choice but to forgive me. Luckily, no advocate around to see I'm messing with his son's diet. The advocate has stepped up our training, we now practice every second day under his supervision. I don't like it all. Even Adam is quieter when he is around.

On Friday afternoon, Dad tells Adam to leave his bike at our house after our ride. He then takes both bikes into his workshop. While I hold the light, he checks them over – every spoke and gear, bolt and nut. Dad also checks the pressure in the tires with a small tyre pressure gauge. I suddenly realise the enormity of it all. I'm not ready for this. Dad must have picked up on my doubts because he looks up from cleaning Adam's bike. His blue eyes all serious.

"David – you have trained hard for this. For months, not just two weeks. You are ready. You can do this." He smiles at me. "Remember: you are a Miller. We plan, we train, we execute. Everything will be fine."

"Yes, Dad."

I want to believe that with my whole heart.

Year 1; Month 7; Week 31

Captain David Zacharias Log
Stardate 71562,1 Log Entry 144. Week 31.

D-Day St Michael's Pilgrimage
St Michaels – This is it! It is finally happening. I am so
scared.

It is early, the sun has yet to rise, but the heat is already pressing down. It is going to be another bright, hot summer's day. We, as in family and strangers, are all gathered at the top and along St Michaels Avenue, for today is the day of the St Michael's Pilgrimage and Adam's birthday. The early hour could not keep them away; strangers and family have shown up to watch our pilgrimage down St Michaels Avenue. I look over to Adam, he is a vibrating ball of energy, jumping, touching, always moving. He is wearing his black T-shirt over his G-suit. The T-shirt has a picture of St Michael's church on the front and *Team Miller-McKenzie* on the back in white letters. The T-shirts are courtesy of the Turtles. I was shocked on Saturday morning when the Winnebago pulled up in the driveway. They heard about the St Michaels Pilgrimage from the priest at their church and decided to come for the race on Sunday. Their home away from home stacked with boxes full of T-shirts they are selling with the proceeds going to the church. The Aunties are here too, wearing pearls with their T-shirts. Adam's Aunt Gaby and Uncle Jo are here and both sets of grandparents.

I can see Adam is getting on the advocate's nerves and I take him by the arm and pull him to the side.

"Do you want to know what I got you for your birthday?" Adam vibrates in place. "I'll give you three guesses."

The subject of his birthday present has been off-limits since the advocate heard him badgering me about his gift. Adam takes a peek at the advocate where he is in a serious conversation with my dad but still keeping an eye on Adam. Ms McKenzie is happily helping a neighbour sell early morning coffee, her hair in a carefree ponytail, wearing a T-shirt with a denim. She looks younger and more relaxed.

I have Adam's full attention. "How many questions do I get? Ten? Twenty."

"Eleven, like the number of years in your birthday."

With an eye on the advocate, Adam whispers his first question: "Can I eat it?"

"No, you cannot eat it. You are still on your exercise diet."

He stretches high on his toes, his arms in the air: "Ok. My second question. Can I carry it around, like every day?"

"I suppose you could, but I will not recommend it."

Adam checks on the advocate again. His back is towards us, talking to an old lady wearing a floral hat. "One more, I have one more. Let me think about it." He closes his eyes.

"*Ragazzi*, are you ready? The sun is coming up."

Father Bosinio's voice starts up the butterflies in my stomach. The Father is also wearing a T-shirt with his priest collar; his massive arms thickly muscled and covered in tattoos. We quickly found out over the last three weeks that the Father is more muscle than flab. He is munching on one of Mom's health muffins. We baked nearly a hundred muffins to sell today.

"Yeah, finally it is going to happen." Adam happily scampers away to get his bike. This is it. The Father puts his hand on my shoulder, "You'll be fine, Davey – remember…"

"Faith, Father. I know, but this is a monster of a hill."

I turn to look at St Michael's Avenue – all three-point three-four kilometres of steep downhill. The avenue winds down between vivid purple Jacaranda's with here and there splashes of pink from the Pom-Pom trees and the fiery red of the coral trees. Red and white danger tape flutters in the morning breeze. Dad has arranged for the barricading of the three T-junctions coming in from the north as well as the large intersection a block before St Michaels Church. Father Bosinio has distributed flyers asking for residents to keep their dogs and cats inside and their gates closed from six-thirty to seven. Dad says it is the best time as the sun rises behind the church and would blind us if we go at sunrise. Like a morbid joke, the rising sun lit up the entrance to the cemetery, turning it a bright, gleaming white.

"Davey?" Dad is standing next to me with Firefly. Dad has washed and polished her, she sparkles in the morning sun as if on fire. I take a deep breath and reach for my bike. The next moment Dad pulls me close for a hug, I can feel Mom's arms gathering me close. Their hug makes me feel warm and safe – I do not want to let go, but I do.

"Thanks, Dad. Thanks, Mom."

I check that Firefly is in the right gear, secure my helmet one more time, pull on my gloves, and finally settle on my bike. Next to me, the advocate is giving last-minute instructions to Adam, who is clearly not listening to a word.

Ms McKenzie to the rescue: "Have fun, Kiddo, and come back safely. Love you to bits."

She grabs the advocate's hand and starts pulling him away. He takes a few steps but then turns around and comes back to Adam. I can hear him sigh in frustration. The advocate reaches out and touches Adam's helmet. Adam stops fidgeting and looks at his father:

"I'm ok, Father. Really. I'll be good. Promise."

The advocate gives a chin lift and steps back.

"Love you, Dad."

I hold my breath. The advocate just looks at Adam, and then: "Me too, Adam, me too."

Adam and I turn our bikes around and retreat to the only flat area on St Michaels to begin our pilgrimage. I have a last look around. Mom and Dad, standing hand in hand. Amelia is waiting at the church. Liam is fiddling with the controls of his drone – a paramedic leaning against a tree, Sunny in a black T-shirt and red pants. Sunny? Next to her is Jennie, holding something white in her hands. When she sees me looking, she opens her hands, I recognise the red and white waving cat that brings good luck in Chinese culture. Jennie, with the little *maneki-neko*, starts a warm glow in my chest. She's here! She has come to see me race! I want to go over to her, but there is no time. I give her a quick wave; my hands are shaking, my breathing fast. I look over to Adam, my fearless friend. He gives me a thumbs up.

"Ready, *ragazzi*?" One look at Adam's face and the Father has his answer. He puts his massive hands on our shoulders and learns forward to say a quick prayer for us. I cannot comprehend the words. I listen to the rumbling cadence of his voice; smell the coffee on his breath, his spicy aftershave. I say my own quick prayer – please God, do not let Adam die on his birthday.

Father Bosinio steps away, cups his hands, and using his church voice, shatters the early morning silence: "Faith, *ragazzi* – GO!"

Adam gives a yell and takes off – a bird set free. I do not remember starting off after Adam on his dark blue Raleigh bike. I do not remember the silence and the cheering that followed. I do remember that somewhere on that down-hill to St Michael's, all the knots loosen up and I, David Zacharias Miller, live in the moment. The wind rushes past my ears, my legs pedal strongly, nothing holding me back anymore. I catch up with Adam and move in alongside him. He smiles, eyes back on the road.

We race down St Michael's together. Flying, bend low over our bikes, tyres singing on the road, people cheering, dogs barking.

"Go, Little Nuke, make like a rocket!"

For once, I do not mind hearing my nickname. Happiness makes the world bright, beautiful, and the waves of cheering and clapping sweep us along, over the first T-junction, the second. I smell the sweet honeysuckle, the sun in my face – I want this moment never to end.

The advocate used to make us walk the route, week after week. At the time, I thought he was mad. Every time we walked, he will point out landmarks; danger points; sights; smells. Now I understand; once I smell the honeysuckle, I know there is a slight dip in the road and a little further, a tree trunk lifts up the left side of the road. I angle to the right so that both of us can clear it.

Closer to the third T-junction, there is an area where pigeons congregate, large brown and grey ones. The advocate ordered us to speed down the sidewalk so that the pigeons would fly up with a loud rush of wings, making us instinctively cover our heads with our arms. It made him angry. "No, eyes on the road. They are much faster than you, keep it steady, and hold your line, they would avoid you."

He made us run down straight for them over and over again until we stopped flinching when they flew up in front of us.

I can see the pigeons pecking away in the grass, I move over to the centre; Adam follows. The pigeons fly up with a whirring of wings.

"Steady, keep it steady, hold your line."

I hunker down and ignore the birds. Adam's gaze is fixed on the road ahead.

The round-about is coming up. I fall back a bit to give Adam space to go into the turn; I can hear him working the breaks.

"Gently on the breaks!"

We make it safely out of the round-about, the final straight end of St Michaels leading to the cemetery lays open to us. Seconds later, we clear the slight kerb at the entrance of the cemetery – we are home.

Adam skids smoothly to a halt in front of the tall St Michaels statue in the cemetery, I follow a close second later.

He pulls his helmet from his head, "Davey, Davey, we did it! We really did it! It was amazing! Don't you think it was amazing? Mind-boggling absolutely fantastic!" He does a little victory dance his arms punching the air.

The next moment Amelia and the twins are all over us, kissing, hugging, congratulating. My legs feel like jelly, I collapse down on the raised pedestal of the statue. I look back the way we have come and struggle to believe it is real. I suddenly realise with a bit of sadness that our big adventure is over.

"I love it. I want to do it again. Davey, do you think they will let us do it again?"

"Not today, Adam. Not today." He looks wistfully back on our adventure. "The day is already fully booked, remember? After church, there is a birthday party we need to go to. With lots of presents."

Adam's eyes lit up. "I hope Father Bosinio will have a short sermon. Do you think the choir will sing? Perhaps your mom will sing again. Does your mom sing at home, like all the time? Do you sing, Davey?"

"That was awesome, Dude. What are you going to do next?" Liam puts the drone down and unclips the camera from my helmet. "What is your next project?" We stare blankly at him. "Your next adventure. Listen, I might have some ideas." He has Adam's full attention.

I let the words wash over me – for now; I simply want to enjoy the moment. Burn it into my memory.

I, David Miller, have achieved what I set out to do. I'm Fat Boy no more.

TABLE OF CONTENTS